I0772914

Missing in Missouri
A Missing Mystery, Book one

Helen Gray

ISBN-13: 978-1-965352-16-8

*These things I have spoken unto you, that in me
ye might have peace. In the world ye shall have
tribulation: but be of good cheer; I have overcome the
world.* John 16:33

Chapter 1

Corrie Wright didn't know what to think
when she looked out the window and recognized the
two men emerging from vehicles that had just parked in
front of her house, an SUV behind a police cruiser. She
went and opened it to face the chief police and the high
school principal.

"Hello." She directed her gaze at the police chief,
who had been her husband's superior at the department,
and was a personal friend. In uniform, he was tall and
muscular, with a ruddy complexion and flinty blue eyes
under thick brows.

But her muscles tightened at sight of her former
boss. Handsome and well-built, Nolan Porter had salt
and pepper hair similar to hers. About her age, he wore
neat black slacks, a tan shirt, and a black blazer. He had
been her superior before she retired from teaching and
coaching at the school nearly three years ago.

She stepped back and widened the door opening. "Would you like to come inside?"

Chief Drexel nodded and stepped forward. "We'd like to discuss something with you."

They followed her into the living room and found seats, the chief on the sofa, and Nolan in the glider rocker. Corrie sank into her recliner, somewhat rigid, with her hands clasped in her lap.

Dan, as she and her husband knew the chief, gazed directly at her. "Corrie, we've had a new development in the case of Mr. Porter's missing daughter. Her car has been found."

Corrie stifled a gasp, her gaze darting back and forth between the two men. Nolan's daughter had been in her second year of teaching music at their local high school when she and a male student had disappeared. It happened only weeks before Corrie's retirement at the end of that school term. "Did you find Nola?"

A pained expression crossed the chief's face, while one of agony etched Nolan's. Dan shook his head. "A group of teenagers were out at a camp site on Black River, doing some scuba diving over this past Labor Day weekend."

Corrie understood. It was their last big hoorah time before buckling down to their studies, even though school had started a week and a half ago. What she didn't understand was why she was being informed about it in this manner.

"They found a sunken car that has been identified as registered to Nola."

"I say this is proof she and that male student didn't run away together like everybody said," Nolan interrupted, leaning forward, arms braced on his thighs.

"Something happened to them. We want you to help us find my daughter and that boy."

That boy, Scott Miller, was a basketball player who had been so adept at shooting three point baskets that the students had nicknamed him Swish.

Corrie glanced at the chief, and then back at Nolan. "How? What can I do?"

"Sign up to substitute teach at the school," Nolan interjected, shocking her.

The chief nodded. "We need someone inside the school who can ask questions and look for information that law enforcement wouldn't think about or know how to find. Nolan thinks people would be open with someone with your familiarity with the school and staff.

"You've proven in the past that you can ferret out information," Nolan pressed on. "I know you were instrumental in investigating and stopping the student hazing that was going on at the school where you taught before returning here to teach in our hometown. I've chatted with your former principal at conferences, and he speaks highly of you. He said he hated to lose you back then, but understood your decision to return to your hometown."

And look how I was eventually treated here, she couldn't help but think. But it was history now.

Red Ridge, Missouri was home, and she had needed a change of environment and to be near her parents at the time. Battling leukemia, her dad had died a year later. Her mother now lived in a senior housing apartment next door to her sister on the other side of town. Corrie tried to stop by for a visit at least once a week.

"Are you committed to any kind of job?" the chief

asked.

Corrie shook her head. "I haven't made any plans. This is just so out of the blue that I can't think. I hadn't meant to take another job, at least for a while," she added, even though she was somewhat adrift since her husband's death sixteen months ago after a long battle with cancer. She had planned to take a year or two to regain her equilibrium and decide how she wanted to work her way out of limbo before making any commitments. It would be presumptuous to think she could solve a case that the police hadn't been able to resolve.

"Subbing would only be part-time," Nolan continued persuasively. "And I can place you anywhere you want to be. I could have already retired, but I haven't done it because I can't bear to leave the school before knowing what happened to my Nola."

He needed closure. Corrie understood that. It had been nearly three years since Nola Porter and Swish Miller had disappeared after the big homecoming game and post-game party that early spring night.

"Nothing else has gotten answers, so it's worth a try," the chief said. He can get you access to any part of the building or grounds, or anything else you need. You were still on staff when Nola and Swish disappeared and know the staff members who are still there, which Nolan tells me is most of them. During your husband's years on the force, he told me that you worked campus security during college and took some criminal justice courses. I also know you gained a lot of familiarity with police and investigative procedures and have self-defense training. All that makes us think you might be able to dig up info from inside. Will you at least consider it?"

Corrie stared out the window, remembering those awful days, weeks, and months after Nola and Swish disappeared. She had thought her principal's daughter was doing well as a teacher, and had served as Corrie's assistant with the team, especially valuable in workouts. She owed Nola. No matter how much coolness had developed between her and her principal, she sympathized with his grief. He had lost his daughter—and been through so much since then.

And, yes, she had a desire to know what happened. Maybe it was time to climb out of her despondency and find a new purpose in life. She heaved a deep breath and met Dan's gaze. "I'm not sure I can help, but how about I think and pray over it for a couple of days, get used to the idea, and give you an answer by Sunday evening?"

They both nodded and stood.

"Thanks for that much," Nolan said, his tone apologetic. "I understand your hesitancy, but I'm hoping we can put the past behind us. There are things I regret, and think you're the best person to float around in the school and discover any missed information. You get along with the staff, and the students respected you. With your history, people would be more open with you."

When he extended a hand toward her, she placed hers in it. And, in light of their strained relationship, was startled at the unexpected warmth that ran up her arm. The look on his face told her he was just as disconcerted. "I'll do my best," she said, extracting her hand quickly.

"I'll contact you," the chief said.

She crossed the room and opened the door. The September air that drifted inside was still quite warm, but growing cooler daily.

As she watched the two men climb into their vehicles and drive away, she wrestled her feelings. Did she really have a choice? Could she possibly find answers others hadn't?

She didn't know. She had to, though. The fact that she had a daughter who was a teacher—and had lost a child—gave her an additional level of empathy. She truly wanted to know what happened to those two people, though. And if it was something bad, which she strongly suspected, she wanted to see that justice was served.

Show me what to do, Lord.

~

As Nolan Porter drove away from Corrie Wright's house, he wished he felt more hopeful of gaining her help. She hadn't been overjoyed at seeing him. And he couldn't blame her.

He should have been more supportive during her final year on staff. She was a good teacher and coach, and he should have stood by her rather than letting his wife's interference cause hurt and strain between him and Corrie.

His only excuse was that he had been hurting and not his normal self. But she had been dealing with a seriously ill husband. He should have been more sensitive.

His wife had grown up in St. Louis, a little over a hundred miles north. They had met in college, married, and settled here when he was offered a position teaching math. Shelly had opened her own photography studio and established herself as a town leader.

Red Ridge, located in the southern part of Missouri, was his hometown, and it hadn't changed a lot since his youth. It was a simple lifestyle, a quiet town surrounded by farms. The school, three manufacturing plants and a hospital were the major employers.

Typical of most small towns, everyone in Red Ridge knew practically everybody else, and those who were "somebodies" had a tendency to flaunt their control over anyone who did anything they didn't like—such as supporting someone in the wrong on an issue because they were a friend or relative.

The church he attended, sporadically rather than regularly like in the past, stood at the end of Main Street, which was occupied by a Wal Mart, a grocery store and a string of smaller businesses and fast-food places. The post office was located on a side street a block over.

Tree leaves fluttered at each side of the road in the late summer-early fall breeze as he drove beyond the city limits to his larger than needed house in a nice subdivision. A minute later, he pulled into his garage and shut off the SUV's engine. Then he sat there, staring ahead and thinking about Corrie.

He had wondered about her after she retired to take care of her terminally ill husband, a respected police detective of longstanding. He had attended Kent Wright's funeral a year and a half ago, and then six months ago he thought he had spotted Corrie in a back pew at his ex-wife's funeral. They were both alone now. But he had been alone for a long time before Shelly's death.

Shelly had been only a year older than Corrie, but they had been totally different in natures, temperaments, and personalities. While his wife projected an image of style and sophistication, Corrie depicted wholesomeness and self-assurance, and she still looked much younger than the fifty-five he knew her to be.

He had been caught up in career advancement, earning his masters and specialist degrees, and then becoming the principal when Doug Green, the former principal, retired from the position, and failed to see how his wife had become more and more focused on being friends with the "right" people and growing in self-importance and somewhat dictatorial.

Corrie, on the other hand, truly cared about her students and the school, as well as her own family and the people around her. She may have taught and coached sports, but she was smart and also taught science and biology. She was also observant and analytical.

She was the only person he could think of who had a decent chance of helping him figure out what had happened to his missing daughter. He hoped she would agree to try.

Chapter 2

Monday morning, Corrie exited the school administration building and drove down the hill to the high school parking lot. Friday night after Dan and Nolan's visit, she had not been able to sleep. Toward morning she had dreamed. In her weightless, suspended state, she had seen an angel standing beside her bed. And the heavenly being had said, "Do not be afraid, Corrie. You have been chosen."

Then the image disappeared.

Corrie had then wakened with a sense of purpose. Her Bible study group was currently studying about angels, a subject that had always fascinated her, which could explain her dream. But she couldn't shake the sensation that a teacher and student had been unjustly accused—or much worse. When memories of newscasts and articles she had heard and read about teachers and students running away together crept into her mind, she forced them away. But she couldn't reject what seemed an angelic message and opportunity to help seek justice for them.

The first thing she had done Saturday morning was to call Chief Drexel and tell him she had reached a decision. And this morning she had added her name to the sub list. Her aim now was to find Nolan and let him know. She pulled into a vacant spot and parked.

When she stepped inside the front office, she saw that Rose Lutes was still at the reception desk. The middle-aged woman looked up, and then smiled in recognition. "Well, good morning, Coach Corrie. What are you doing back on the premises?"

"I'm looking for Mr. Porter. Is he in?" She tipped her head toward his office door.

"No, but he's in the building somewhere. I'll let him know you're here." Rose picked up the phone and dialed. "Coach Corrie is here to see you," she said moments later. "I'll tell her."

She disconnected and looked back at Corrie. "He's on his way and said for you to have a seat in his office."

Corrie had barely settled in the chair facing his desk when Nolan strode through the doorway, closed the door and rounded the desk. "Dan said you called him and said you'll help us. Thank you," he said, taking a seat.

"I agreed to *try* to help you," she amended. "I'm still not sure what you expect of me." *Or what kind of support I can expect from you.*

Nolan leaned forward on the desk, his intense dark eyes boring into her. "I expect—rather I hope—to restore the good working relationship we had before I let my wife run roughshod over my life and relationships. I should have supported you more fully." He paused to press his lips together and take a breath before continuing. "Can you forgive me and let me prove that I trust your judgment? And not just because I need your help," he added quickly.

She studied his expression and rigid neck muscles. He was obviously uncertain about her response. She decided to give him the benefit of the doubt. She could sort out her feelings and level of trust later. "It's in the past. And I share your desire to find answers. What do you want me to do? Is there a plan?"

The tension visibly drained from him, his hands unclenching. "Thank you. I don't really have a plan. Can we just start at the beginning, as if there was never an investigation, and see what we can learn? I feel like our different perspectives on the personal lives of Nola and Swish, especially here at the school where they spent so much of their time, should be helpful. There *has* to be something the police missed—something important—that someone here can tell you."

Corrie couldn't imagine what the police would have missed that she could find, but she appreciated that Nolan seemed to think she could. He needed closure. So did she. And she needed to feel useful. Here was her chance. So she asked the first question that popped into her mind. "Has Swish's truck ever been found?"

Nolan's right fist bounced on the desktop. "No, it hasn't. And the fact that Nola's car was found in the river makes me think his truck must also be out there somewhere. And just like I've always said, they did not run away together. Yes, I know that kind of thing has been known to happen, but it didn't in this case. And I need to prove it."

Corrie nodded. "I agree. I think they need to do some more diving. I'll call Dan when I get home and see if that's already being done. Do you know who first suggested that Nola and Swish ran away together?"

He grimaced. "I'm not sure. You know how easy it is for rumors to start. And it's literally impossible to figure out where that one started."

"It might not be a bad idea to see if I can trace it."

His fist bumping slowed to a halt. Then he inhaled deeply and smiled. "You're already thinking like an investigator, and I have confidence you'll figure out who to ask."

"Do you know who saw them last?"

He nodded. "They had both been at homecoming that Friday evening. Nola was still putting away equipment in the band room when the students left the gym after the end of season basketball game, heading for the post-game party out at the youth center. The janitor, Henry Jones, said he saw her there a little after nine o'clock. No one that I know of knows exactly when she left the party. And no one thought anything about it until she didn't show up for school Monday morning."

"Does Henry still work here?"

Nolan nodded. "He does, still on the evening shift."

Corrie made a mental note to talk to Henry. Cleaning staff saw a lot of behind-the-scenes stuff that no one else noticed. "What about Swish? Who saw him last?"

"According to the police, he and some of the team members left the party early and went joy riding. There was some drinking involved, but the guys all said they came back to the gym later, where they split up and went their separate ways. No one remembers seeing which way Swish drove away from the building."

Corrie had been heartbroken over those

disappearances, but she had also been such an emotional mess over her husband's deteriorating health condition and the decision to retire early that she hadn't absorbed as many details as she normally would have done.

"What about dating? Were they each seeing anyone regularly?"

Nolan nodded. "Swish dated several girls, but the current one was Rochelle Crocker."

"What has she been doing since graduating from high school?"

"The last time I heard, she was attending college in Cape Girardeau and working part-time in her mother's law office."

Corrie recalled that the girl had been quite involved in school activities, including cheerleading, but she had seemed more interested in her social life and good times than academics. Rochelle had shown athletic ability and played volleyball her freshman year, but quit the team when the workouts became more demanding. It had also been a tumultuous time in the girl's life, with her parents divorcing and her older brother entering the military.

"What about Nola? Was she involved with anyone romantically?" Corrie asked, redirecting her thoughts.

Nolan shrugged. "I don't know how involved they were, but she had dated Eric Tomlinson a few times. There had been a serious romance during college that didn't end well, so she wasn't particularly interested in anything serious at the time."

"Eric was a couple of years older than her, wasn't he?" Corrie remembered both from their years as high school students.

Nolan nodded. "She was twenty-four when she disappeared, so he would have been twenty-six, making him twenty-nine or thirty now. I heard that he married recently, but I'm not sure where he lives. I think he works out of town."

A bell began to ring, and moments later the sound of students filling the hallways between classes could be heard. He stood. "I need to get out there and keep an eye on a couple of students who have been feuding."

"Do you have a class schedule handy that I could have?" she asked, also rising. "I'd like to know when teachers have their free periods and would be available for conversations."

He reached into a desk drawer, snatched a form and handed it to her. "Welcome aboard, and don't hesitate to talk to me about anything. I mean that," he added, opening the door.

Corrie nodded and walked ahead of him. They parted at the hallway. She headed to the exit, scanning the schedule she held. She stopped when she saw that Piper Randall, the business teacher, had this next class period free. Piper was not only a colleague, but she was a close friend who possessed techie skills far beyond Corrie's abilities. She had also been a homecoming sponsor the year Nola and Swish disappeared.

~

As Nolan turned the corner into the north hallway, he spied Corrie veering away from the exit and heading toward the stairwell. It didn't take a genius to deduce that she was on her way to see Piper. He hoped she enlisted her friend's help.

He also hoped she would overcome her distrust of him and prove the ally he thought she could be. She was an attractive woman, brown-eyed, with touches of white in her short dark hair, a look that young girls spent a fortune having artificially created. Her creamy skin also belied her mature age. Tall and physically fit, she had been a high school and then college volleyball player.

He admired the way she had grown stronger over time and done everything she could to take care of her husband during his long battle with cancer. He also knew that Kent had frequently used her as a sounding board when wrestling police cases.

His wife had also changed over time, but Shelly had become driven toward success and status. He had to shoulder some blame. Too caught up in his own job, he had not given her as much attention as he should have. He regretted that.

Then their world had fallen apart when their daughter disappeared. Shelly had demanded that he find Nola, and then blamed him for everything when he couldn't. She had turned bitter and tuned him out. Then she had gone to Florida and moved into a house near their son and spent a great deal of time at Nick's.

Being blamed for Nola's disappearance had hurt.

Shelly's leaving him had hurt.

He didn't think he could be hurt any more, but when his son called last year and said a stroke had incapacitated Shelly, he had hurt more. And her death six months ago had nearly destroyed him.

After the funeral, he had been surprised when his daughter-in-law mentioned Shelly saying she thought the shop teacher had killed Nola. He needed to tell Corrie about that.

Chapter 3

Corrie waited at the end of the hall until it cleared. Then she went to her friend's still open classroom door and peeked inside. "You open for visitors?" she called softly to Piper's back as she returned to her desk.

Piper spun on her heel, and then beamed in recognition. "Corrie? It's so good to see you." A hug ensued. Then Piper leaned back to study her. "What are you doing here?"

Corrie smiled. "Stopping to see you, of course."

Piper laughed. "I'm glad. It's been too long. How are you doing?" She gestured toward a chair.

Corrie settled onto it and waited for Piper to be seated. Then she folded her hands in her lap and stared directly at her friend across the desk. "I've agreed to something that may be way beyond me, but I think my chances would be better if I had the help of an old friend."

Piper leaned forward. "I'm intrigued. How can I help you?"

Corrie hadn't asked Dan or Nolan if she could take Piper into her confidence, but they had indicated they trusted her instincts. And Nolan certainly knew

Piper's abilities and insights. She drew a deep breath.

"I know you'll have students soon and don't have time for a long conversation, so for starters would you think back about the homecoming three years ago and write down everything you can remember? Since you were the lead sponsor, you spent way more time than anyone at the game, post-game party, and everything else that went on that evening."

"Wait a minute," Piper said, coming upright in the chair. "Are you digging around in that cold case?"

"Would you call me crazy if I said yes?"

A contemplative look came over Piper's pixie-like face, and then a grin slowly curved her mouth. "I'd say it's time somebody did, and I think you're perfect for it. Are you on your own, or is there more to it?"

"Dan and Nolan have asked me to sign on as a substitute teacher as an excuse to float around the building and see if I can stumble into any information that might shed light on the case."

Piper turned solemn. "I think that's a good idea. I'll search my memory bank and list everything I remember. Of course, you know I've been questioned before and told the police everything I knew."

Corrie nodded. "I know. But Nolan wants to start over, as if there was never an investigation, and see if we can find any new angles."

"It's been so long. I can't imagine what new info we can find."

Corrie liked hearing the *we* description. "There is already something new. Some teens out scuba diving in Black River this past weekend found Nola's car."

Piper gasped. "And Nola?"

Corrie shook her head.

"Then she must be dead," Piper said quickly.

The same thought had already been keeping Corrie's gut tied in a knot. "If that's the case, there's a killer out there. And he or she needs to be brought to justice for it. And Nola needs to be found."

"Do you think Swish could have done it?" Piper's face had gone pale.

Corrie's head rotated back and forth. "I don't know what to think. Would you be willing to use your techie skills and search for any kind of connection between them?"

"I'll do whatever I can to help," she said, glancing up at the clock. "I'll work on some memory notes tonight. The rest will have to be done as I can find time."

Corrie stood, knowing students would be flooding the room within moments. "Let's don't make any overt announcements about my presence in the building— even though I'm sure it won't take long for word to get around when I start asking questions." She grinned.

Piper rounded the desk and gave her another hug. "Let me know anytime I can help. And I'll immediately let you know if I stumble across anything relevant."

Corrie thanked her and left the room. She marched down the stairs and headed for the exit. As she reached it, Nolan came from the front office and motioned for her to stop.

"Do you have time to meet me at the police station when I can get away from here, which should be about 3:30, and ask Dan if we can read over any of the old police reports he feels he can let us see?"

She considered the timeline, and then nodded. "I can do it." Before then, she wanted to see if she could find Eric Tomlinson or Rochelle Crocker.

He gave her a thumbs-up, said, "Thanks," and took off down the hall as the bell began to ring.

Once home, Corrie searched the phone book and then online for addresses for Eric and Rochelle. When she drove to the address she located for Eric, she found the home vacant. And no one was home at the apartment listed for Rochelle. Neither was a surprise, since it was a working weekday.

What a beginning to her investigation. Corrie sighed, walked away from the apartment building and drove home. After a quick lunch and running some errands she went meet Nolan at the police station.

When she pulled into the parking lot and recognized Nolan behind the wheel of a dark blue SUV, she parked in an empty spot two vehicles over from him. He came striding toward her as she emerged from her white minivan.

"I called Dan, and he's expecting us," he said as they met. "He said he'll have the files out that we can read."

When they entered the reception area, the woman at the front desk smiled in recognition. "The chief is waiting at his desk for you."

The office they entered hadn't changed since Kent became too ill to work any longer and left the department. Corrie sat on one of the two chairs facing Dan's desk, and Nolan took the other.

"Was anything significant found in Nola's car?" Corrie asked, anxious to hear any new developments or information.

Dan grimaced. "There was an extra pair of tennis shoes in the back seat, and the glove compartment held the usual small items, including what looks like evidence of paperwork having been in a leather packet, but nothing that indicates she was packed to leave town."

"Someone killed her," Nolan groaned hoarsely, his shoulder muscles quivering. His obvious pain made Corrie's own heart ache.

The grim look Dan aimed at her said he couldn't dispute the statement. "We're doing all we can to find out what happened to her," he assured Nolan.

"Are you doing any more diving in the river, looking for the boy's truck?" Corrie asked. She remembered seeing Swish driving a truck on the school parking lot.

He nodded. "We are, but we haven't found anything yet. The young men who found Nola's car have volunteered to search other areas where young people sometimes hang out for parties and such."

"Is that the police report?" Nolan indicated the folder in front of Dan, his jaw rigid.

Dan pushed it toward the front of the desk. "It's as much as I can share with you. But I assure you there's nothing else that would help you."

Corrie let Nolan start first and pass pages to her as he finished reading them.

That long ago Friday after school, Nola had helped the band students clear the stage of chairs and music stands used to play before the game and at halftime and return them to the band room. She had still been there when the students all left, but she had attended the party later as a chaperone. An eyewitness had seen her going to her car with a couple of tote bags as people were leaving the youth center located across the street from the school, where the party had been held. And that was the last anyone remembered seeing her.

After she was reported missing, teachers and students had been interviewed and a grid search done of the areas around the school and youth center.

The police had canvassed the route Nola normally drove to her apartment from school, and checked with businesspeople and residents all along that two mile stretch. But no one recalled any accidents, cars with flat tires, or anything unusual. It was estimated that she had vanished somewhere between 10:30 and 11:00 that Friday night, since she had not been seen over the weekend.

Nothing had stood out in Nola's phone records, and her Facebook account revealed no students in her friends list, something teachers were not supposed to do. But where her usage of the social media site had been irregular, Swish's had been heavy. He had played a lot of online games.

Nothing was found in either phone or computer that yielded clues as to the whereabouts of the two. Updates indicated there had been no action on Nola's credit card since she disappeared, and her driver's license had expired and never been renewed.

~

Nolan was in agony as he and Corrie walked out of the police station, fighting the fog of hopelessness that had settled over him. The years of memories, the endless days and weeks of praying that his daughter would one day walk through the doorway, had taken a toll on him both physically and emotionally.

"We'll find answers," Corrie said beside him.

He glanced at her familiar features, and the hint of a smile she gave him had an odd effect on him. As he shook it off, he remembered what he had meant to ask her. "I hope you're right. Would you consider attending school on the pretense of subbing tomorrow, but float around and talk to different teachers during their free time?"

She paused on the sidewalk and faced him. "You mean go undercover?" Her mouth twitched slightly.

He shrugged. "I guess so. If anyone asks who you're subbing for, you can tell them whatever you think works. Get creative and avoid the question as much as you can."

"Is there anyone in particular you want me to talk to first?" she asked while resuming motion.

He kept pace with her. "Yes, there is. After Shelly's funeral, my son's wife said that Shelly told them one time that she thought Greg Briley killed Nola. There's nothing I've seen or heard that supports that, but ..." Greg was the industrial arts teacher, commonly referred to as the shop teacher.

"You'd like me to chat with him and see how he reacts to questions about her," she finished for him when he paused.

He nodded. "It's probably a waste of time, but we need to start somewhere."

She approached her car door and turned to face him. "I'd like to know who the last person was to see Swish. I don't think the two ran away together, but the fact that they're both missing tells me there's some kind of connection."

"Coach Lorimer is pretty close mouthed about his basketball players, but you worked with him at times and knew him well. Maybe you can get him to talk about Swish's former team members from that year."

She nodded. "That's good thinking. I'll track him down."

Chapter 4

Corrie entered the school building toward the end of first hour classes the next morning, having deliberately arrived late so the halls would be empty. After checking in at the office and making a nod of acknowledgement at Nolan as she passed his open office doorway, she walked down the hall, exited the building and continued up the sidewalk to the separate building that housed the band room and industrial arts classroom. She knew from the schedule Nolan had given her that the shop teacher had no class this hour.

When she entered the shop room right after students had exited from the just finished class, she was met by the sight of work tables loaded with hand-held tools and benches where hydraulic and power tools sat.

Greg Briley, a tall man about forty years old was a veteran teacher who exuded an air of confidence acquired through his years of successful teaching, craft fairs, student projects and elaborate projects for private customers. The man looked up from examining a hand-powered tool. When he recognized Corrie, he put the tool down and came toward her, a look of puzzlement on his face. "Hello, Coach Corrie. Are you coming back on staff?" His tone was pleasant enough, but his smile didn't quite reach his eyes.

"Just subbing," she said casually, offering no details as sounds of band instruments warming up carried from the other side of the building. "May I chat with you for a bit?"

Greg's look of puzzlement took on a touch of guardedness. "I get the feeling you have a particular topic in mind. What is it?"

Corrie motioned at a couple of chairs against the wall. "I want to know your impression of how well Nola Porter got along with other staff members." Now seated, she set her purse on the floor by her feet.

Greg angled the other chair to face her and plopped onto it. "Are you digging around in that case?"

She wasn't sure how to answer. She didn't want to lay out the full truth, but she couldn't lie. "I'd like to know what happened, as I'm sure her family would, and I'm sure Swish's family also would."

His head nodded slowly. "And what you'd particularly like to know is how Nola and I got along. Is that right?"

She shrugged. "Being the only two teachers in this smaller building would make you better acquainted with her than any other staff."

His mouth tightened. "Am I hearing some kind of accusation in that?"

"Not from me."

"Who then?"

She saw no alternative but the truth. "Before her death, Nola's mother is reported to have said she thinks you killed Nola."

Greg's eyes rolled, and his face tipped toward the

ceiling. "It figures." He lowered his face, his head moving side to side. "That woman saw trouble behind every door frame. Thank goodness, her husband is nothing like her."

"What about their daughter?"

"Nola and I got along fine. She was more like her dad than her mom. But you know what gossip mills workplaces can be, including schools. I suppose I can see how someone might make a crack about the two of us being the only adults up here in this building and twist it into something it's not."

"What about her relationships with other staff? Were there any petty feuds?"

That brought a quirk to his mouth. "We both know those happen, don't we? Like when another teacher accused the FACS teacher of stealing for taking food home with her. Is she just supposed to throw all leftovers in the trash?"

Corrie nodded understanding.

"The same teacher—we both know who we're talking about—accused Nola of improper behavior with a male student," he continued. "They were clearing the stage after the band had played at a ballgame during half time, and as they were leaving the stage, Nola tripped. A male student grabbed her, probably saved her from breaking her neck. Everyone saw it, but one person interpreted it differently and spouted off about it. I avoid that teacher."

Corrie knew that most teachers did. "I'm afraid she's going to end up with no friends at all if she doesn't change her behavior."

"She was new while you were here, but she's run her course since you've been gone," he said with a note of satisfaction. "I've heard she's due for tenure this year, and I'm betting it won't be granted."

It was time to change the subject. "What about Swish? Did you ever have him in class?"

Greg nodded. "I did the year he was a junior. He didn't seem to like it all that much, but he didn't give me any trouble."

"What about his behavior with the other students? Do you know if there were bad feelings between him and any of them?"

Greg frowned. "I didn't observe any. Sometimes he was rather cocky, but he didn't harass others in class. Coach Lorimer keeps his players in line and always knows them better than anyone else does. I'm sure he could tell you more about them—if he will."

Corrie glanced at her watch and stood. "Thanks for the chat."

He grinned—a bit tongue-in-cheek—and walked with her to the doorway. "Am I going to be seeing you around?"

She managed to maintain a pleasant expression. "I'm on the sub list."

"Good luck," he called as she headed down the sidewalk.

She pulled out the class schedule and scanned it as she walked. Coach Lorimer didn't have the next class period free, but he did the following one. She would use this hour to find Nolan and relate her chat with Greg.

"What's up?" he asked when Corrie entered his office.

As she took the seat in front of him, she noted the softening of his tone as he spoke to her. And there was the tinge of a smile on his face. Maybe he had meant it about wanting to restore their working relationship.

"I'm just stopping by to let you know I talked to Greg Briley." She went on to relate their conversation. "He didn't give me the feeling that he's hiding any bad vibes between him and your daughter."

Nolan leaned back in the chair, his hands forming a steeple in front of his chest. The flecks of silver hair at his temples increased his attractiveness. "I never really thought there was, but it was a place to start your questioning."

"I don't think Greg bought my implication that I'm here just to sub."

Nolan grinned. "I don't really care. You're officially on the list, and I officially want you here. Continue the role, and let those who suspect your motives think what they please. They should all want answers."

Corrie glanced at her watch. "I'd better get moving if I'm going to catch Coach Lorimer before he can leave the gym at the end of this class."

Nolan nodded. "Go get him, Tiger."

Corrie left, enjoying the more relaxed air between them. Then it hit her that being a sub meant he was once again her superior. She squashed the thought.

She waited at the gym door until students stopped exiting and then entered. Inside, Rick Lorimer eyed her from across the large room. He held a basketball in his right hand and wore an expression that was hard to read. There was recognition, of course, but was there also a hint of suspicion? He waited for her to approach him rather than coming to meet her.

"Are you lost?" he asked as she approached him. His face was thin, nearly to the point of gauntness, and his hair had quite a bit of gray in it, but he was still a handsome man after twenty some years of teaching and coaching.

Corrie shrugged, shaking off memories of hours spent in this gymnasium. "I ran into Mr. Porter recently, and he said he's short of subs. So here I am."

A slight grin crossed Rick's ruddy face. "So you had to stop by here just to smell the sweat. Right, Mrs. Wright?"

She grinned back at him. "I admit I've missed it."

His expression sobered. "Enough to sub? Or is there more to it?"

She shrugged. "I came to see if you'll chat with me a bit."

He frowned. "What about?"

"Nola and Swish's disappearance."

His head moved slowly back and forth. "It's hard to remember that, much less talk about it. Why would you want to discuss it now?"

"I've been wondering about them," she said vaguely.

He pointed at the bleachers. "Let's have a seat."

They moved to the bottom bench and sat side by side. "Why now?" he asked.

She set her purse beside her and faced him. "Because it's been too long since the matter has been talked about, and I guess being married to a detective for so long makes me want it checked into some more. Second looks pay off sometimes."

He studied her for several more moments. "You don't think the teacher and student ran off together?"

She shook her head. "They didn't let anyone know anything, they didn't take anything with them, and there has been no action on Nola's credit card or other records. Her car was found in the river this past weekend," she added, watching his expression.

Rick's eyes rounded. "You're sure about that?"

"Yes," she said without elaboration. "What can you tell me about Swish, besides what is common knowledge? If Nola's car didn't leave town, I'm afraid his truck didn't either. And if their vehicles didn't leave, I'm sure they didn't. And their families need answers."

Rick took a deep breath. "Swish was a bit high on himself, but he was a good player and followed my rules."

"How well did he get along with other students when he was in your classes?"

"Okay, I guess. Of course, he had certain ones he hung out with, while pretty much ignoring others."

"Did he keep his grades up just for the sake of sports, or did he need help?"

"So far as I know, he did his own work. He was a bit short tempered at times, though, and expressed his dislike for some of the classes," he added in slow thoughtfulness.

"What about his friends? Were his pals exclusive to the basketball team, or did he run with another crowd?"

"It was mostly the team, at least so far as I know."

"Do you know where they hung out away from school?"

Rick's jaws puffed with air as he exhaled heavily. "They were told to keep decent hours and stay away from booze and smokes, but teens like to experiment and party."

"Which players did you consider Swish's best friends?" She remembered that year's team, but not a lot about their personal lives and habits. She had been so stressed over Kent's health and whether to retire early that she hadn't paid as much attention to student social activities during her last couple of years on staff.

"He and Jason Martin, Taylor Daniels and Wade Dabney spent a good deal of time joyriding on weekends."

Corrie remembered something from the police reports. Wade Dabney had been the eyewitness who saw Nola heading to her car after the post-game party. But instead of mentioning it, she asked, "Do you know where those three boys are now?"

"As I'm sure you know, Wade is a deputy here in town. Taylor works part-time at the local grocery store and attends college classes at Three Rivers. Yeah, it's only a junior college, and he's never been real keen on academics, but he takes a couple of classes each semester, probably to satisfy his parents. Jason attends SMSU at Cape Girardeau full-time, but they're both usually in town on weekends." He grinned. "I think they mostly come home to bring laundry to their moms and get free home cooked meals. But they both work Saturdays at the grocery store." Jason's parents owned the local supermarket.

He glanced at his watch. "It's been nice chatting with you, but I really need to take care of a couple of things before my next class."

Corrie grabbed her purse and stood. "I've enjoyed it, too. Thanks for your help."

"Will I be seeing you around?" he asked as she started to walk away.

"You can count on it," she called back over her shoulder.

Chapter 5

Nolan liked the way Corrie had jumped right into the investigation. Now he needed to step back and let her proceed on her own. But he didn't want to do that. Even though their relationship was tenuous, he wanted to know everything she did and learned.

He had let his wife alienate Corrie, so he couldn't hover over her or do anything to damage whatever ground he had regained. He was fortunate that she cared enough about Nola and Swish to get involved, which he suspected she would have done years ago if her personal life had not been so stressful at that point.

He reached for his phone, but paused when the office secretary appeared in his office doorway. A classroom crisis claimed his attention. By the end of the day he had decided where he wanted Corrie to focus next. He returned to his desk and called her.

"Hello," she answered. "What's on your mind?"

"I was wondering if you've done any more, uh …"

"Snooping?" she supplied when he hesitated.

He grinned at her light tone, his nerves relaxing. "Yeah."

"I went looking for Swish's joyriding pals," she

said with no overtone of resentment.

"I assume particular friends?"

"Yes. Coach Lorimer said he hung out with Jason Martin, Taylor Daniels, and Wade Dabney on weekends."

Nolan leaned back in the chair. "Did you find them?"

"I caught up with Taylor at the grocery store, and he confirmed that Wade is the eyewitness who saw Nola going to her car the night she disappeared. Then he clammed up and wouldn't talk to me anymore."

"The police are certain enough that he wasn't involved in whatever happened that they hired him as a deputy, but that doesn't mean he doesn't know something."

"I agree," she said. "I'm scheduled to sub for Monica Reynolds Friday. You'll be dismissing early that afternoon, won't you?"

"Yes." Every year the district did that the Friday before the fall festival weekend so students could spend the afternoon working on their floats for the Saturday morning parade. "And that brings me to the purpose of my call. I'll be keeping an eye on float preparation, but I think the festival would be a good opportunity to talk to more people. Do you plan to attend?"

"Sure. It's a tradition, and I wouldn't miss it. It's a chance to chat with old friends and former students."

"Would you want to watch the parade with me Saturday morning and see how our school float entrants do?"

When she didn't respond immediately, he feared he had made a mistake. "I'll watch, but you don't ..."

"I can do that," she said before he could

backtrack.

After ending the call, he sat staring across the room. Corrie's willingness to help him made him feel guilty for not being more helpful to her during her tough times—and allowing his wife to ride roughshod over her. Although he had apologized, and Corrie had said it was in the past, it still bothered him. He owed her.

~

By mid-morning Saturday, the sun had chased away the early morning chill. Corrie and Nolan parked side by side in a restaurant parking lot near the edge of town. Wearing jeans and sweatshirts that were comfortable in the air that was crisp but stimulating, they sat in lawn chairs in front of their vehicles to watch the parade.

Before long they heard the sound of a siren that signaled the fire engine leading the parade was near. Behind the truck, a color guard and the high school flag team marched, while behind them the drum major and majorettes tossed batons in the air ahead of the band. The snappy cadence of the drums made Corrie's feet itch to high step to it.

As the procession continued, they watched an array of floats representing the school, as well as churches, scout troops, community and business organizations, roll past them. There were also local celebrities and dignitaries. And politicians.

Corrie came upright in the lawn chair as a particular vehicle passed in front of them. Rochelle Crocker marched alongside the car bearing a political billboard proclaiming the candidacy of her mother for an open municipal judgeship.

Nolan looked over at Corrie. "I assume you want to talk to Rochelle?"

She nodded. "If they're campaigning, they're bound to have a booth on the festival grounds. I didn't realize Mrs. Crocker had political ambitions."

Nolan shrugged "I didn't either. I mean, I knew she's a lawyer and that Rochelle is working part-time in her office while attending college classes in Cape Girardeau, but not too many public defenders become judges."

"I guess she plans to beat the average."

Corrie returned her attention to the parade. When it ended, they folded their lawn chairs and stowed them in their vehicles.

"Parking spots are going to be hard to find at the grounds," Nolan said to Corrie from across the bed of his pickup. "Why don't you ride down with me and leave your car here? I'll bring you back after we've made the rounds and had something to eat."

She saw the wisdom of his plan. It took several minutes to drive across town to the city park in the snail-paced moving traffic, then several more to find a parking spot. As they exited Nolan's truck and walked to the lawn where the carnival spread out over the grounds, Corrie suddenly became self-conscious about being seen in public with Nolan.

He was the principal, and she was a retired teacher, once again working under his authority. And they both had only lost their spouses within the past year or two. Well, Nolan's wife had been his ex and living in another state for a couple of years before her death. And her husband had been terminally ill for so long that his death had been a release from suffering that she knew Kent welcomed. But she was still readjusting—and certainly not interested in any kind of serious relationship with a man, especially this one.

"Would you prefer pizza, burgers, or something else?" Nolan asked.

"Pizza's fine." She veered to the concession on the left.

Once they had their food and sodas, they found seats at one of the tables arranged in groups across the walkway beneath a cluster of trees. Corrie bowed her head and offered silent thanks to God for the food. When she opened her eyes, Nolan was staring across the table at her. "I'm afraid I haven't thanked God for much in a long time."

"I understand. I also know that the Bible says we will have tribulations, but that we should be encouraged because He has overcome the world, and our sorrow will turn to joy."

He frowned, his head motion negative. "I can't see any joy in my circumstances."

"I admit that life has been tough, but I cling to God's promises."

Help us, Lord. Give us comfort. And answers.

As tension eased out of her, Corrie focused on eating. "Shall we stroll over the grounds?" she asked when they finished.

"We may as well," he said, gathering debris from the table and tossing it in the nearest trash can. He waited for her to walk in front of him back onto the walkway.

They had only gone about a hundred feet when Corrie spotted a booth with the name Alicia Crocker displayed in big bold letters on a large sign. Rochelle stood to the left of it, handing out flyers to anyone who would take them.

The young woman was about five and a half feet tall, and her hair hung long and straight to her shoulder blades. It had been bleached and tinted to a light gray color that older women went to great pains and expense to achieve. Her makeup and fashionable blue dress made her appear older than the twenty-one-or-two that Corrie knew her to be.

"It's a beautiful day for this," Corrie said to Rochelle as they approached, hoping to initiate a conversation. She noted the mother, Alicia's, presence behind the long table that fronted the booth, stacks of flyers spread over it. She was speaking to an older gentleman.

Rochelle's gaze darted from Corrie to Nolan and back. "Imagine seeing you two together," she said in a voice that seemed friendly, but tinged with criticism. Rochelle extended a flyer to each of them. "Help us put a competent judge in office."

Corrie studied the sheet, noting the professionally produced photo of Alicia Crocker. In her late forties, the woman had dark hair with artificial highlights streaking it. Today she wore a fashionable navy pant suit and several pieces of jewelry.

"Are you aware that my daughter's car has been found?" Nolan asked.

Rochelle's startled reaction said the question had taken her by surprise. "I read the story in yesterday's paper. Has she been found yet?"

"No," he responded brusquely. "But it proves to me that she didn't run away."

Behind them, Alicia waved good-bye to the man

she had been talking to and rounded the table to stand beside her daughter. "I heard you mention Nola's car being found."

Nolan nodded. "The teens who found it while they were scuba diving in Black River, along with law enforcement, are now searching that area for Swish's truck."

"I hope they find it, as well as your daughter and the young man."

Instead of responding to the mother, Nolan focused on Rochelle. "I know you dated Swish. When was the last time you saw him?"

The young woman frowned. "The police questioned me after he disappeared."

"I'm sure they'll be questioning you again now that's there's new evidence," Nolan informed her.

She stood in thought for several more moments. "I saw him leave with some friends after the homecoming party. I expected him to come back and pick me up to go hang out and have a soda together, but he never came."

"You have my deepest sympathy," the mother said, offering Nolan a handshake. "I wish I could help you, but I have no idea what I could do. If you'll excuse me, I have people waiting to speak to me."

They resumed walking the circuit of booths, rides and concessions, and had headed back to Nolan's vehicle when Corrie spotted a familiar face at the kettle corn concession up the walkway a bit on the other side of it. He was wearing a police uniform, but she was sure of his identity. "There's Wade," she said, veering across the lawn. Nolan kept pace with her.

"Hey, Wade," she called as they wove their way

through the busy crowd.

Wade turned, his features passive as he searched for the source of the call. When he spotted them, his eyes rounded in recognition.

"We'd like to talk to you," Corrie said as they approached him.

Wade's body seemed to go a bit rigid. "I know about Nola's car being found. If that's what you want to talk about, there's nothing new I can tell you."

"But you know other things," Nolan said, now beside Corrie. "Don't you want my daughter and your friend to be found?"

"Of course I do," the young deputy said. "But I don't know anything that can help. I told the police everything I knew back then, and I'm not assigned to the case now."

"Let us ask you a few questions anyhow," Corrie interjected. "We know you and your friends were all questioned years ago, but this discovery puts a new light on things."

He nodded. "As a police officer I know that, but my answers will be the same."

"But new details could come to light when there's new evidence," she reasoned.

"We understand that you saw Nola going to her car the night she disappeared. What was she carrying?" Nolan asked.

Wade swallowed, obviously finding the memories unpleasant. "Just a couple of bags of stuff and a big purse hanging from her shoulder. I saw her going across the parking lot, but I didn't watch her get in her car."

"Were you close friends with Swish?" Corrie asked.

Wade shrugged. "I guess as close as any of the rest of the players."

"Did you get along outside of school hours? Were there problems or fights among them?"

An odd look flashed across his face.

"What is it?" Nolan pressed. "I know Swish was never in trouble for fighting in school, but did he anywhere else?"

Wade's Adam's apple bobbed, his eyes darting side to side in a way that sent an odd tingle up Corrie's neck. She suddenly recalled something. "I once saw Swish sporting a bruised and swollen jaw. Who did he fight with?"

Wade shook his head. "I don't know."

"Look, I know that a sports team is a tight brotherhood, but if there was friction among the team members that year, we need to know about it," Nolan said firmly.

"All I remember," Wade said, hesitating slightly before continuing, "is hearing Swish make a comment one time, something about making some money at the fights. But it was only that one time. Then he clammed up, and I never thought any more about it. If you have any more questions, you'll have to talk to the chief. I'm sorry, but I have to go. I'm on duty."

Corrie watched Wade walk away, and then resumed walking toward the park exit with Nolan. She wasn't sure what she had gotten into, in addition to a missing persons case. But the man beside her suddenly seemed different from the man she had worked alongside for years. Something about Nolan, and the atmosphere between them, had changed. Become more empathetic. And scarily intriguing.

Hopefully they could be friends, teammates in the search for his daughter, but nothing more. Nolan and the police chief had indicated they trusted her instincts, but how would Nolan respond if she made a decision he didn't like?

Chapter 6

Sitting in church service Sunday morning, Corrie's attention had begun to drift, but she came alert when the pastor's words suddenly penetrated her brain.

"Learn to do well; seek justice, relieve the oppressed, plead for the widow," he quoted from Isaiah.

The "seek justice" part was what had jumped out at her. As she reflected on it, a sensation crept over her that God was looking favorably on their search for justice for Nola and Swish.

But the pastor's words continued. "Seeking justice is okay, but we must be careful that we are truly seeking justice rather than revenge. Perfect justice must be found in God's courtroom, not our own. So we must trust Him for guidance."

Corrie silently prayed for God's guidance and placed the matter in His hands. She also prayed for comfort and strength for the families of those missing.

When the service ended, she joined the line of people filing out the door of the church where the pastor stood shaking hands. Across the room she spotted Wade Dabney walking toward her, but he slowed and veered to a side door. The action was subtle, but it still gave her the feeling she was being avoided.

"It's nice to see you again so soon."

Distracted, Corrie hadn't noticed Nolan stepping from a pew into the aisle next to her. She hadn't noticed him earlier, so she assumed he had arrived a bit late. They had both attended this church for years, but interacted only casually, keeping their work relationship at work. Then he had become erratic in church attendance after his daughter's disappearance, and stopped altogether after his wife left him.

"It's good to see you here," Corrie said, not wanting to press, yet welcome him back. Hopefully he would find strength and comfort in Christian fellowship and worship.

She didn't know quite how to evaluate the relationship between her and Nolan, but they were certainly united in their desire for answers. She did, however, wish that they could be friends, the kind who completely trusted one another.

Before either of them could say more, Shirley Evans, an older member of Corrie's Bible study group, approached them. "I heard about Nola's car being found. Does that mean the police are closer to finding out what happened to her?"

The question to Nolan was direct, but genuine caring colored the woman's tone. Shirley was a prayer warrior, not a gossip. And Corrie assumed Nolan knew that.

He drew a heavy breath. "I'm not sure. I think it means they're seeing that she didn't run off with a male student. They're investigating further."

Shirley nodded. "That's good. You've been in my prayers all this time. It's good to see you here."

Corrie and Nolan exchanged glances as the woman walked away. "We're blocking traffic," he said, stepping closer to Corrie's side. "Would you be interested in having something to eat with me and then driving out to the river to look at the spot where Nola's car was found?"

Corrie wasn't sure going to a restaurant with him was a good idea, but a trip to that spot in the river was intriguing. "Okay," came out of her mouth before she could rationalize further.

He smiled and stepped back into the aisle. "Let's go in my vehicle, and I'll bring you back for yours when we're ready to go home."

After shaking hands with the pastor and his wife at the door, they exited the building. Once in Nolan's SUV, Corrie eased back in the passenger seat. And found that sitting next to Nolan in the enclosed vehicle was comfortable—too comfortable.

"What kind of food sounds good to you?" he asked, pulling out of the parking lot.

She considered the choices available in the town. "Barbecue or Chinese both sound good," she said, leaving an option.

He shot a grin over at her and steered left onto the highway. "You said barbecue first, so let's do that."

At the door of the restaurant, Nolan took her arm in a polite gesture and guided her to a table. That she liked his touch surprised her.

Once they were seated and had placed their orders, Nolan leaned back in his chair, arms folded across his chest. His expression became sober. "You're a straightforward person, aren't you, Corrie?"

She shrugged at his serious tone. "I've been

known to state my mind rather frankly. Have I said or done something that's bothering you?"

The corners of his mouth tipped upward slightly "You've been you. And you seem to be overlooking my failure to stand up for you against Shelly's interference years ago."

"I don't see any point in dwelling on history that would only stir up hard feelings and hinder our search for truth."

"I appreciate that, but I'd like to explain a little bit," he said, sounding a bit tense. "Shelly and I had begun to disagree on more and more things, and I didn't want to fight with her. When we attended that tournament and those two girls squabbled and created a disturbance, I should have backed you in disciplining them. Instead, I kept quiet at Shelly's insistence that Rochelle's lawyer mother would sue you for wrongful punishment, even though you were correct in benching them."

"We're living in an age of litigation, unfortunately," she said diplomatically. "And I understood at least some of the pressure you were under at the time." He had also been dealing with disagreements on multiple issues among school board members, including some regarding their sports programs.

"Thank you for being so generous. I knew you were fair and treating those girls the way you would any students, including those whose parents aren't powerful control freaks."

When he went silent, she studied the contemplative look on his face. Was there more on his mind?

"I want to be forthright with you about something else now," he said, answering her question.

"Spit it out," she said, still studying him.

He leaned forward, his arms on the table. "I always felt we had a good working relationship, but now something seems to be different. I'd like to keep things strictly on business between us, but it's suddenly not as easy as it's always been. There's a sensitivity developing between us, at least on my part."

She stared at him, folding her arms over her pounding heart. So she hadn't been imagining things. "Do you want me to stop hanging around the school?"

"Oh, no," he replied instantly. "I asked you to help with this investigation, but I felt I should warn you about this new …whatever it is."

She ran her tongue along her suddenly dry lips. "Are you saying that you want to keep our relationship to only friends?"

He heaved a breath and pierced her with a sharp gaze. "I think that's how things should be—until the case is resolved."

Corrie felt her cheeks flush. She slowly released her breath. "And after?"

"It could possibly change then—if you're comfortable with the idea."

Suddenly her pulse rate accelerated. She swallowed. "Kent told me months before he died that he didn't want me to mourn him too long, but to move on with my life after the grief settled. But I couldn't see ever having another in my life. And it's so soon."

He nodded. "When the time is right, maybe things could change. Why don't we leave it at that?"

She tipped her head, studying his sincerity. "I

think it's a good idea."

The arrival of their order ended the conversation.

~

Nolan's fists clenched as he and Corrie stood on the boat dock at the edge of the Black River, staring at the out-of-the-way site where Nola's car had been found.

Black River ran in the Ozark Mountains of Missouri and flowed in a southeastern direction to Poplar Bluff before entering the White River near Newport, Arkansas. The course was two hundred and eighty miles.

A breeze created a slight ripple in the water, and the mid-seventies September temperature was pleasant. But the river was the normal black color for which it was named. His thoughts were more like the black water than the pleasant weather.

"Dan said the keys were still in the ignition, and it was in gear," he said in a near growl. "It was deliberately run off this ramp, not an accident. The windows were up, so it floated out there." He pointed to a point a few hundred feet out in the water.

Corrie followed his thinking. "Does viewing this give you any ideas about where she could be?"

He frowned and shook his head. "I wish it did— had hoped it would. But the only thing I can think is that this is a party spot for the sport teams—and others. Some of those activities go on all night long."

"And I'm sure there are things happening that shouldn't," she added.

His head motion changed to a nod. "If she was abducted and brought out here, someone had to have seen or heard something. But who? And what?"

When Corrie's hand came over his in a sympathetic gesture, his chest tightened. It had been so long since anyone had shared his pain in a way that touched him deeply.

"Children bring us such joy …and heartache," she said softly. "I know how hard it is to lose one." Her voice quavered a bit.

Nolan turned to face her, creases forming between his brows.

"Jordan was a preemie," she continued softly. "But he was a fighter. Against all odds, he survived and came home. And he thrived for two years. Then he …"

Nolan held his breath when she paused in an obvious effort to regain her composure. He hadn't known. "Was this before you returned here to teach?"

She nodded and drew a deep breath. "He was a happy child, and we loved him dearly. He laughed and hugged us and gave us so much joy. Then we lost him. He died peacefully in my arms after sudden heart and lung failure. I still miss him."

She understood more than he could have imagined. Empathy went beyond sympathy. She had experienced it. The age of a child didn't matter. If lost, your heart broke. Instinctively he placed an arm around her shoulders and tugged her rigid body to him in a gentle embrace. Yes, friends could share such things. The loss of a child was a unique bond, heartbreaking, but comforting in knowing they truly understood the pain. "There are no words," he murmured, giving her a hug.

Then he stepped back, not wanting to overstep any bounds of their freshly established friendship. "Where did you live when all that happened?" he asked, wanting more insight into her life. They had both grown up here, but had never dated one another, and had gone separate ways after high school. After they both ended up on the staff at the high school, he had worked with her professionally, and was even friends with her husband, but he had never known much about her life between the time they both graduated from high school and left for college and when she returned to teach at the school. And he had never heard her mention losing a child.

"Jefferson City," she responded, stepping over a rut in the ground. "Kent and I met when my college volleyball team was playing in a tournament there. He was a city policeman who happened to be off duty and attending the games with his brother to watch his niece play. One night there was a fender bender on the parking lot after the game. Some teens had been partying, and a couple of them rear ended our team bus. The impact threw me backward, and I hit my head on the back of the seat so hard I nearly passed out."

Nolan winced at the image her story produced. "Were you hospitalized?"

"No, Kent called an ambulance to have EMTs examine me, but I recovered quickly, with the help of some Tylenol."

"So how did your relationship with Kent develop?"

"He was at the next morning's game, and he asked how I was feeling. We ended up having a nice chat and refreshments at the concession stand between games. Then he asked if he could call me later to check on me."

Nolan grinned. "So you gave him your phone

number, and then you became more than friends."

She nodded. "Since he already had a job there in Jeff City and was about to be promoted to detective, when I graduated, I found a teaching position there. It's where we began our married life. Jordan was born after Kayla and Jeremy. When we lost him, we struggled. So we prayed and asked God to show us how to move on with our lives. Soon after that, I received a call asking if I would be interested in coming home to teach and coach. And the police department had just budgeted for a full-time detective on the force here."

"So you saw it as a new beginning," he said, phrasing it as a question.

"One provided by God. Did this trip give you any ideas?" she asked, changing the subject and heading back to the vehicle.

"No, but it's made me more determined to keep pressing for answers," he said, keeping pace beside her. "*Someone* knows what happened and where Nola is."

"We'll dig until someone talks."

Her determination-laced words gave him hope.

When he pulled in at the church and parked next to Corrie's car, she exited and headed to her own vehicle. He backed up, turned toward the exit and drove several yards ahead. Then he glanced in his rear-view mirror to see if she was following him.

To his shock, he saw a figure wearing a ski mask and baggy pants emerge from the far side of the building and run straight toward Corrie, a baseball bat clutched in one hand.

Heart pounding, he shut down the engine and bolted from the car. As he ran toward them, Corrie broke into a run across the lot. Her assailant followed and swung the bat at her head, but she jumped sideways and took a blow to her shoulder, tripped and fell.

Suddenly she let out an ear-splitting shriek and sprang to her feet. Then she kicked at her attacker, sending his feet out from under him.

As Nolan ran within feet of them, the guy scrambled to his feet, took off running and disappeared around the building. Nolan took off after the hoodlum, but he was too late. The roar of a motorcycle sounded from behind the church, and then went roaring away before he could get close enough to see it.

Chapter 7

Corrie's land line phone rang at five thirty Monday morning. She reached over and grabbed it from the bedside table. "Hello."

"This is Rose," the school secretary said. "Your successor called in sick this morning. Can you cover your old routine?"

"I guess I can try, and see if I'm still up to it," she mumbled sleepily.

"Okay, see you soon."

She hadn't slept well last night. Nolan had called the police, and they had been questioned. But she hadn't been able to tell them much about her assailant except that he had been tall and slight of build, but quick on his feet. And she didn't know why it happened. Did the fact that he carried a bat mean he meant to rob her—or hurt her?

Two and a half hours later, Corrie inhaled the familiar scents of the locker room and eyed the desk where she had spent so many hours during her years doing this job. The sights and smells stirred memories of spiked volleyballs and the rhythmic pounding of basketball players running drills.

When the bell rang, she hurried back out to the

gym to monitor students as they entered. One of the teenage girls paused when she spotted Corrie. Then she grinned and veered to where Corrie stood in front of the bleachers.

"Are you subbing for Miss Rogers today?"

"Yes," Corrie said.

The teen stepped closer. "I'm Dina Eaton, Naomi's younger sister. She still talks about how much she loved playing volleyball for you. And I loved watching those games."

Corrie smiled, remembering. "Naomi was an excellent player. What about you? Are you on the team now?" She hadn't kept up well after retiring to take care of Kent.

Dina grinned. "Of course. I love it. But I would have loved to play for you." Her tone softened. "Naomi was sick about the disappearance of Miss Porter and the Miller boy during her senior year."

Corrie nodded. "We all were."

"Miss Porter was another favorite of Naomi's," the girl continued. "I remember her laughing about how much she loved playing in the band and marching in the parades. Some of her stories I remember best are ones about how they used to sneak into the storage room to eat snacks."

At that moment the final bell rang to start class. As Dina hurried to the locker room to change into her gym clothes, Corrie followed and peeked in at the activity. Then she returned to the doorway to listen and watch as students returned to the gym floor for class.

Wearing tennis shoes and sweatpants, Corrie slipped back into her old routine, conducting exercises and keeping score while the girls played volleyball. She was too busy to ask questions of them, and most were too young to have been in high school then.

Moments after the bell rang to dismiss for lunch, Piper entered the gym. "I have two sandwiches and Cokes, if you'd be interested in sharing them with me," she called as she made her way across the floor.

Corrie grinned and pointed toward the locker room. "I assume this means you don't have lunch duty. Come on back to the desk."

Piper grinned, looking around as she settled onto a chair near the desk. "This is like old times. I love it." She set the sandwiches on the desk and pushed one of the Cokes toward Corrie. "When I heard that you were here this morning, I thought it was prophetic that I had packed an extra sandwich."

As they ate, Piper updated Corrie on staff turnover and workplace scuttlebutt.

"Was Swish ever in trouble?" Corrie asked when they finished eating.

Piper frowned. "I don't think he ever did any time in ISS or anything like that, but I've heard he ran with some rough characters away from school. He was good looking and had a way with the girls. I'm sure he got away with a lot. And his dad gave him a truck and let him do pretty much whatever he wanted. Have you done any more investigating?" she asked in a sudden change of subject.

Corrie told her about the previous afternoon's visit to the river.

"Did it provide any insight into the case?"

"It gave us a better picture of how the car was put in the water, but not why, or by whom. It's frustrating."

Piper studied Corrie for several moments. "I think

you're going to figure it out. And I want to help in any way I can. How has your day back here in the gym been?"

Piper's abrupt changes of subject tended to give Corrie mental jerks, but she also enjoyed the rapid coverage of topics. "It's been kind of fun. Some students, including Naomi Eaton's little sister, have been very welcoming to me."

"Wish I had time to stick around longer," Piper said, rising. "But the bell is going to ring in about sixty seconds. If I run, maybe I can make it to my room before the halls are full of students."

After Piper left, Corrie went to the gym doorway to greet the next class. The afternoon was routine, but her thoughts kept wandering back over the day. And the conversation with the Eaton girl kept rising to the surface of them. Visions of Nola's school environment, the band room, accompanied those thoughts.

Could that storage room possibly contain anything significant?

What would it hurt to look?

After the last class of the day had ended and the gym emptied, Corrie left with the intent of asking Nolan to let her into the band room.

She was halfway to the front doorway where she expected to find him when she spotted the evening janitor coming toward her up the hall that was already nearly empty of students. Nolan stood at the point where the hallway intersected with the main entrance/exit.

Corrie aimed a pointed look at him and made a head motion toward the janitor to indicate she wanted to talk to Henry. Nolan responded with a nod and moved on down the hallway, checking each way for lingering students.

She veered over alongside Henry, whose attention was focused on the floor and the mop bucket he was pushing. "Hi, Henry."

When the janitor paused and looked up, his eyes rounded in surprised recognition. "Well, if it isn't Coach Corrie," he said in his slightly raspy voice. "What are you doing back here?"

She grinned. "I missed you and the gang. How are you?"

He shrugged. "Gettin' close to retirement. Some tell me it's not all it's cracked up to be. Is that what happened to you? Did you get bored and come back to work?"

"I was at loose ends a little bit," she admitted truthfully. "But there were other factors as well. We both have a lot of memories in this place."

He nodded.

"May I ask you something?"

"Sure." He pushed the bucket over next to the wall.

"What are your memories of the disappearance of Nola Porter and Scott Miller?"

Henry ran a hand over his scruffy mop of nearly gray hair. "I remember about the talk and how upset and worried people wuz."

"We were all upset and worried."

Henry eyed her more piercingly. "Are you pokin' around and asking questions for a reason? Like trying to find them two after all this time?"

Corrie nodded, counting it pointless to deny it. "There's been a new development. Nola's car was found in the river."

His eyes narrowed. "Have you figured out how it got there? Or is that what you're tryin' to do?" He smirked.

Corrie didn't bat an eye. "Do you remember anything that might help me do that?"

A hand rubbed back and forth over the bristly surface of his chin, and his brow crinkled in thought. "Like I told the police back then, the last time I remember seein' Miss Porter was when she was leavin' the band room just before the homecoming party at the youth center." As he finished the statement, his brow crinkled in thought

"What is it?" she asked. "Have you remembered something else?"

"Well, yeah," he said slowly. "I saw her another time, but it was before that, so probably means nothing."

"When was it?"

"Earlier in the evening. She was walkin' toward the parking lot, and her boyfriend was with her."

"Do you mean Eric Tomlinson?"

He nodded. "Yeah, that was him. He sometimes met her after school when she stayed late. I figured they were going somewhere to eat together before the game, but they didn't."

"What do you mean."

"Well …their hands wuz movin' as they talked, and when they got to her car, she faced him with her arms crossed and said something. Then she got in the car, and he took off across the parking lot."

Corrie frowned. "It sounds like they were arguing. Did you hear anything they said?"

"No. I was up here at the building, and they wuz nearly to the edge of the lot when I noticed 'em leaving the sidewalk. Never thought no more about it."

It was probably a dead end, but she needed to follow up on it.

Henry glanced down at his mop bucket. "I better get going if I don't want to end up retired right now."

"I'll take full blame for your five minutes," she said, knowing he was joking.

"Did you have an interesting chat?"

Nolan's voice at her shoulder startled Corrie as she watched Henry push his bucket down the hall. She turned to face him. "It was interesting."

"Why don't you tell me about it while we go find some pizza?"

She liked the idea, but hesitated. "Do you think it's wise for us to hang around together so much? Some might consider it unprofessional now that I'm working at the school."

He shrugged. "There's nothing wrong with friends hanging around together. And we have a common cause. But we can eat at the Pizza Palace if it'll make you feel more comfortable."

It was in a nearby small town, and they served the best pizza in the area. "That sounds good." As she said the words, she recalled her other purpose. "Would you mind visiting the band room with me first?"

Twin furrows formed between his brows. "Is there something else you need to tell me?"

"Not really. This morning a student mentioned how her older sister and her friends used to hide snacks in the band storage room and sneak in to eat them. I've been in the band area numerous times, but never in the storage room. I'm just curious."

He nodded. "Sounds like when I wanted to look at the river. Let's go."

~

Nolan stared at the pictures attached to the wall of the little storage room. A sense of devastation mingled with pride in his lovely, talented daughter. The photos were of her or her with individual students, with groups, or with the band in uniform. Sight of that decorated wall brought memories that overwhelmed him. Nola as a baby. As an elementary student. As a teen. And then as a teacher. She had just been getting launched in her teaching career, learning to balance relationships with students, staff, administration and parents, when she suddenly disappeared.

Where are you, sweetheart? What did someone do to you?

He had avoided this classroom as much as possible. Nola's absence was felt so much stronger here than any other place in the building. And there had never been a reason for examining this small section of space where the walls were filled with shelves that held instrument cases—all except this end wall that was covered with images of Nola.

"It's a lovely memorial," Corrie said softly.

He nodded, swallowing against the constriction in his throat. "I don't know how the students located some of those pictures, but the act shows they cared about her."

"They still do," Corrie assured him. "The pictures were probably put here the year she disappeared. But they're still here. And I suspect some have been added over time."

When she clasped his hand, he returned the pressure. He hadn't realized how special Corrie truly was. She was not only willing to forgive his shortcomings, but she meant to help him in his search for his daughter. He wanted to cry, but he couldn't.

The conversation with Henry that she had related while walking to this room returned to mind. "You said Henry saw Nola and Eric arguing. We have to talk to Eric."

Chapter 8

The twelve-mile drive in Nolan's SUV to the pizza buffet involved more quiet introspection than actual conversation. But that changed once they were seated in the restaurant with salads and plates loaded with pizza slices before them.

When they raised their eyes from the brief blessing Corrie offered, Nolan seemed to relax a bit. His expression was thoughtful. "My daughter's name is obviously a form of mine. What about yours? Is there special meaning to it?"

She grinned. "My mother was a huge admirer of Corrie ten Boom, to the point that she named her only daughter after the woman."

He smiled in return, which was good to see. It didn't seem to happen much. "So is your name actually Cornelius like hers?"

She shook her head. "No, it's just Corrie. It's what ten Boom was known as all her life. Mom said if it was good enough for ten Boom, it was good enough for me. She was a brave woman who was credited with saving the lives of about eight hundred Jews. I'm honored to be named after her."

"You're right," he agreed, his expression somber.

Corrie sipped from her iced tea. Not only had she lost a child, but her daughter was a teacher. It was a double bond between her and Nolan that brought fresh waves of understanding and sympathy. "I know you were so proud of Nola. And I'm sure you also are of your son."

"Nick is doing well as the sales manager of a large corporation. And he makes more money than I ever did—or will."

They each ate a slice of pizza before Corrie resumed the conversation. "Do you have any idea why your wife would think the shop teacher killed your daughter?"

Pain flashed in Nolan's eyes. "I don't. It doesn't make sense. Nick said his mother never told him or his wife her reason for blaming Greg Briley. We'd better eat this before it gets cold." He picked up a slice of pizza.

When they were back in Nolan's SUV, he started the engine and faced Corrie. "After I drop you at your vehicle, I plan to make some phone calls, see if I can find out where Eric is living now."

She nodded, also anxious to talk to Nola's former boyfriend. "Will you call me if you locate him?"

"I will. And when I'm ready to visit him, you're invited to go along."

As he put the vehicle in motion, Corrie's thoughts shifted. "Did your wife know the school staff well?"

"She knew who they all were, but she wasn't personally acquainted with everyone. She basically knew everybody in town, though."

Everyone who rated knowing, Corrie thought a bit cynically, and then felt bad about her poor attitude.

"Shelly became depressed and bitter after Nola disappeared," Nolan said as he exited the parking lot. "She demanded that I find her, and I wasn't able to do it."

"You couldn't be expected to do what no one else, including the police, could do."

"I felt like a failure, though. And when Shelly said she was done with me and left, I felt even worse. But I couldn't follow her—even if there was a chance of reconciliation. I had to stay here and keep looking for my girl."

"Shelly went to Florida, didn't she?"

He nodded. "She lived near our son—and divorced me. Not long after that she had a stroke that paralyzed the entire right side of her body and damaged her speech. Nick had to put her in a care facility, where she spent several months before her death this past spring."

Corrie's heart ached at all he had endured. "Answers are out there. We just have to find them." "I had lunch with Piper in her room today, and we looked at her yearbook for the year of the disappearances. The team starters that year were Swish the power forward, Jason Martin the center, Wade Dabney the small forward, Taylor Daniels the outside shooter, and Chuck Osborn the point guard. And no one knows where Swish is."

He became thoughtful. "Jason is a student at Southeast Missouri State on an athletic scholarship. Wade stayed here, married Cindy Dalton and became a local deputy."

"Wade said he saw Nola walking to her car after homecoming," she said. "But the janitor told me he saw her earlier with Eric Tomlinson, and it looked like they were arguing. And when I saw him at church, I had the feeling he was avoiding me."

"Taylor Daniels was attending Three Rivers College part-time, but I heard he quit," Nolan continued. "Chuck Osborn enlisted soon after graduation. The last I heard was that he's deployed in Germany."

"But he was here when Swish disappeared," she pointed out. "I wonder if he wanted out of sight for more reasons than just patriotism," she speculated.

"This is all interesting, but what does any of it tell us?"

"I'm not sure. And Piper mentioned something that raises another question in my mind. The subject of the missing persons case came up in my accounting class yesterday and someone said they heard that a couple of those players had a serious crush on Nola."

"Are you thinking there was some kind of fight about it?" he asked.

Corrie frowned, recalling Swish's bruised face. "It seems pretty far-fetched."

Nolan also frowned. "Stranger things have happened. I think Dan needs to hear about this, though. He and I have maintained a good relationship over the years, but it has strengthened into a more personal friendship recently. He'll take every detail seriously."

"I'll go to the police station as soon as I leave here," Corrie volunteered.

When Nolan delivered her back to her minivan, she found herself reluctant to part with him. But that was nonsense. She couldn't let compassion morph into anything more. She reminded herself that they were simply friends with a mission for truth and justice.

So why did spending time with him feel so right?

He aimed a measuring look across the seat at her as she undid her seat belt. "Listen, I know we have good cops who did everything they could to find our missing people. But I can't sit back and do nothing. Now that Nola's car has been found, I have to do everything I can to find her. She's here somewhere. I know it. And with you and Dan behind me, we're going to find whatever was overlooked before. There's new insight."

She opened the door, stepped out and leaned over. "I believe you. And secrets have a way of surfacing. Let's find her."

~

Nolan watched her go, his feelings mixed. He welcomed her help, but hated that it had apparently put her in danger. He had to keep a close eye on her, protect her.

He went home and made several calls, inquiring of anyone he could remember being related to or pals with Eric. The young man had never struck him as bad for Nola, nor had he given the impression that he had a hot and heavy thing going with her. Nola had mentioned Eric occasionally, and they had definitely dated a few times. But the fact that they had been seen arguing needed to be explored.

Eventually he learned that Eric had married, lived in a neighboring town and was a long haul truck driver, a job that kept him away from home during the week.

He pulled out his cell phone and dialed Corrie.

"I was hoping you would call," she answered. "What have you found?"

He outlined what he had learned. "Eric is on the road all week, only home weekends. So we're stuck until Saturday, and it's only Monday night."

"We'll just have to wait then."

When the call ended, Nolan felt the tiniest bit of progress. If nothing else, they were actively pursuing the case. That thought would help him sleep a little better tonight.

Chapter 9

When Corrie walked into the police station, the deputy on desk duty paused in a phone conversation and gave her a grin of recognition. "If you're here to see the chief, he's at his desk." He motioned her on back.

When Corrie entered the room, Dan looked up from the folder he was studying. "You look like something's bothering you. Have a seat."

She sat in the chair facing him and related what Wade had said about Swish telling someone he made money at the fights. "Do you know how he would have been making money from fights?" She had a suspicion, but hated having it confirmed.

Dan's chair squeaked as he leaned back in it. His eyes narrowed on her. "When was this conversation?"

She explained about seeing Wade at the festival, not totally comfortable discussing one of Dan's deputies with him.

"He's a good deputy," Dan said, his mouth flattening. "I know what's behind that."

"I'm all ears."

He rubbed a hand across his jaw and inhaled deeply. "We had some parents claim that their kids were being bullied and pressured into fights. Then students would cheer them on and place bets on who would win."

"I assume you did something about it." It shook her to realize how clueless she had been during that time. Her regular job and extracurricular duties had been extremely time-consuming, and then Kent's deteriorating health had required more and more of her time and energy. But she still should have known about it—even if Dan had most likely shielded her. He had also been struggling with Kent's condition. Their relationship had been more than just detective and chief. They had been personal friends.

Dan made a jerky head nod. "We questioned students until we identified a ringleader—I'm sure there were more—and shut them down. Wade was in no way involved, but I can see that he wouldn't want to discuss it."

Corrie drew a breath of relief. It hadn't been a lead, but it had cleared away a question.

"Was that all you had on your mind?"

"Well …there's one other little thing. A student mentioned in Piper's class that a couple of basketball players had crushes on Nola. If Swish was one of them, could that have led to some kind of fight that got one or both of them killed?"

Dan rubbed his chin, his head moving slowly back and forth. "Anything is possible, but it's pretty far-fetched."

"I assume you haven't found Swish's truck yet," she said, changing the subject.

"No, but people are still out there looking. And we've recruited a forensic K9-unit dog and its handler from St. Louis. They're working the thick brush and trails in the area surrounding where Nola's car was found."

"I'm glad to hear that."

"They're not making fast progress, though. The recent rains have created humidity, and that makes it harder for K9 dogs to smell. So they have to take breaks more often."

"Any progress is better than none," she said, glad to hear about the increased efforts.

When Dan's phone rang, Corrie saw no reason to take any more of his time. She stood, gave him a little goodbye wave and left.

But she couldn't drop the matter of teenage crushes just yet. It nagged at her on the drive home and through a light lunch, and then made her attempt to take a nap fruitless. At three o'clock she gave in to the itch, returned to her car and drove back to the school.

Inside the building, she spotted Coach Lorimer in the hallway and followed him inside the gym. He paused and faced her, furrows creasing his brow. "You're back?"

She shrugged. "I have one more question for you. I hope you don't mind."

"I reckon not, but I don't know anything to help your case." He stepped over and dropped onto the bottom bleacher seat. "I'm tired."

She sat beside him and came to the point. "Another teacher heard a student say in her class that two players on your team had crushes on Miss Porter. Do you know anything about that?"

He scrutinized her through narrowed eyes. "You're thinking a couple of students fought over Nola and she ended up dead, maybe from trying to break up the fight. I can't see anything like that happening, even though a couple of those guys did seem to spend a lot of time helping her with band set-ups and take-downs, things like that."

"By any chance was one of those players Swish?"

He made a slight startled motion. "As a matter of fact, it was. He played drums and gave the impression he loved band and would do anything for Miss Porter."

"Who was the other boy?"

Now his expression turned pensive. "It was a good kid who never caused trouble. He played trombone and also liked band. Those two sometimes had trouble juggling their after-class time between their sports and music programs. They were late for ball practice more than once."

He paused, as if reliving those days. "Jason Martin was heartbroken when Nola disappeared. I remember walking into the locker room one day and finding him sitting there crying. There's no way that boy harmed a teacher he respected and adored, or a teammate who was also a friend. He's a guy I still expect to end up in some kind of ministry."

"Well, thanks for letting me take up some more of your time."

"I hope you find the answers," he said as she walked away.

Corrie was just crawling into her car when her cell phone rang. It was Dan.

"Hello," she said, sliding behind the wheel.

"I talked to Wade. I'm still convinced he's innocent of any involvement in the bullying or fighting that was going on back then. But he did admit that there's a personal reason for not wanting to talk about it. He was afraid his younger brother was being bullied and forced to fight. Sean wouldn't admit it, but Wade saw him limping and wearing long sleeved shirts in warm weather. There were also things in his behavior that Wade found suspicious."

Corrie got the picture. "He was covering bruises. Did Wade get his brother to admit it?"

"He said Sean would never admit it, but he saw the bruises and was convinced. He said he became his little brother's best friend. This was back in Wade's junior year. Sean was still in junior high."

"Stuck so close to him the thugs couldn't get to him, huh?" Her impression of Wade had risen as Dan talked.

"That's how I interpreted it. As for Swish and Jason being in puppy love with Miss Porter, Wade wasn't sure. He said he remembers them being helpful to her, but never noticed anything bad. And everyone was upset when those two disappeared. He says he never for a minute believed the rumor about Swish and his teacher running away together."

~

The rest of the week passed in a blur for Nolan. One crisis after another kept him on the run. But he still watched the halls for Corrie. The only time he spotted her was Friday afternoon as she walked past the office window on her way out of the building. He dashed out and caught up to her. "Would you like me to pick you up in the morning to see if we can make contact with Eric?"

She faced him, clutching her purse to her side. "What time?"

"Would about nine o'clock work for you?"

She nodded and resumed walking. "See you."

He spent a restless night, but was at Corrie's promptly at nine the next morning. When he pulled into her driveway, she emerged from the house, locked the door and climbed into the passenger seat before he could exit the vehicle.

"I had another interesting chat with Dina Eaton yesterday while I was subbing for Mrs. Richards," she said when her seat belt was buckled.

He put the SUV in motion. "I'm all ears."

"During lab time in her science class, Dina came over where I was standing and wanted to know if I'm still asking questions about the fighting for money three years ago. I didn't ask how she knew about that, but we both know her mother is related to Coach Lorimer. Dina remembers her sister talking about there being forced fights back then, and people bet money on them. I didn't tell her I already knew that."

"Did she know the police put a stop to it?"

"She didn't indicate she did. But her concern is more current. She said she recently overheard someone make a wisecrack about a kid being flattened at the flats, and when she asked around about it, she was told to forget about it, that someone must have been making a joke."

Nolan's gut clenched as he passed the city limit sign and turned left onto the highway. When they reached the edge of Midville, he turned onto a county road and drove about a mile up it. When he spied a mailbox with the name Tomlinson on it, he turned into the lane and drove to where it came to a dead end at a white frame house. He parked, and they walked up onto the porch. He rang the doorbell.

The man who appeared in the doorway had sandy hair and high cheekbones. He was about six foot three, almost gangly, and looked to be in excellent physical condition. He wore blue jeans and a blue tee shirt.

"Hello, Eric," Nolan said.

Eric appeared startled at recognizing them. "Hello, Mr. Porter …and Mrs. Wright."

"I understand you've been on the road all week, so you may not be aware that my daughter's car was found in the river."

"My wife told me about it," Eric said gruffly, stepping out onto the porch and closing the door. He apparently didn't intend to invite them inside. But he did point at the porch swing and two chairs facing it.

The two men took the chairs, so Corrie sat in the swing seat.

"I hate to bring up the subject of Nola and Swish," Nolan said, understanding that Eric surely suspected that was what they wanted to discuss, and he didn't want to do it in front of his wife. "But we'd like to ask you about something. Someone said he saw you and Nola walking to the parking lot shortly before she disappeared, and you seemed to be arguing. Was there trouble between you and my daughter?"

Eric drew himself up sharply. "That's personal."

"But she disappeared, and now her car has been found. That says to me that somebody did something to her. And I need to know who and what it was." He struggled to speak without losing his temper or emotions.

"It's been three years," Eric said in a tight voice. "What do you expect to find after all this time?"

"After a length of time, people often remember

something new, or something they've kept secret that needs to be shared."

Something flashed in Eric's expression at the last phrase.

Nolan leaned forward. "What is it? Did you remember something? Or is there something you've kept hidden? Was she mad at you? If so, why? What did you argue about?"

Eric just sat there, his darkened eyes staring ahead. He swallowed.

"Whatever it is, be honest with me, Eric. Please."

The guy heaved a tortured breath, and his chin quivered. He swallowed again. "She was mad," he finally said, almost inaudibly. "But not at me."

Nolan frowned. "Then who was it?"

"I can't tell you."

Chapter 10

"You have to," Corrie said as calmly as she could manage.

Eric shook his head. "It doesn't matter."

"Maybe it does," Nolan said, having regained his speech. "Tell us so we can see if it's relevant."

"I can't," he repeated.

For several moments Corrie watched Eric struggle with whatever was preventing him from telling them the truth.

"We need to know everything, Eric," she said, struggling for a balance between pleading and demanding while wanting to drag the full truth from him. "You never know what detail can provide direction in a case. And we need to find the truth."

Eric stared at her, and then at Nolan. Then he took a deep breath, clearly struggling over the matter. Finally, his lips moved. And paused. Then he drew another deep breath. "She was mad at her mother," he said, his voice barely audible.

"What do you mean?" Corrie blurted.

"Why?" Nolan demanded.

"That's the part I don't want you to hear from me," the young man said, clearly upset.

Nolan edged forward on the edge of the chair. "If it concerns my wife and missing daughter, you have to tell me."

Eric's face tipped upward, his eyes blinking. Then he seemed to pull himself together. His eyes focused on Corrie. "She had walked in on her mother and Mr. Briley in his classroom earlier. They were kissing."

Where had that come from? Corrie looked at Nolan, whose expression was not quite as shocked as she would have expected.

"Nola and I were planning to go eat together like we sometimes did after we both got off work," Eric explained. "But she was too upset to eat. So she went on about her duties, and I went home."

"Thank you," Nolan said in a wooden tone. "I can understand why you didn't want to tell me. It may or may not be relevant, but Nola's state of mind had to have been affected. I need some time to think about it."

"I really liked Nola, and I hope you find her," Eric said, coming to his feet.

As Eric reentered his house, Corrie and Nolan headed back to the vehicle in silence. But once they were seated, Nolan faced Corrie. "Greg Briley builds some outstanding craft pieces in his home shop. Shelly purchased a couple of items for the den from him, and she sometimes dropped by the band/shop building to visit with Nola. It never occurred to me that at least some of those visits were with the only other teacher in the building."

"You were busy, and you certainly weren't distrustful of her."

No, just naïve," he said, jabbing the key into the ignition.

"Let's not dwell on that part of it, but try to stay focused on finding Nola," Corrie said. "But we have to wonder if Nola confronted Greg, there was a fight, and he ended up killing her to keep her from blabbing to you, even though the theory is far out," she added.

"It is far out, but I wonder something else," he said as he backed out of the driveway and headed down the lane. "Shelly fell apart when Nola disappeared, and then she abandoned both me and her lover. Could the stress of living with what she had done, plus the possibility it had cost us our daughter, have caused her stroke?"

It was a scary thought, but Corrie's mind had also begun drifting in that direction. "I don't think that's something we can ever know for sure."

Nolan heaved a sigh, his grip on the wheel easing a bit. "Even if that's what happened, what's the connection to Swish?"

"I don't know," she admitted, frustrated.

"You don't think Eric had anything to do with it?" He darted a questioning glance over at her.

She shook her head slowly. "No, I don't. I think he hated telling you that, and he never would have volunteered the information. But knowing points us in another direction."

"Mr. Greg Briley is now a suspect, right?"

She nodded. "We need to share this with Dan."

The drive to the police station was made in silent introspection. When they entered Dan's office, he turned from his computer to face them. "I suppose you're here with more questions—or you have information."

They both nodded and took seats facing him.

"You sure don't look happy," the chief said, studying them.

"We've been to see Eric Tomlinson," Corrie said, wanting to spare Nolan the pain of telling it. "He told us something that makes Greg Briley look suspicious." She gave the chief a quick summary of the conversation.

"I'll be questioning the man as soon as I can catch up to him," Dan said when she finished. "He's among those who provided solid accounts of their time and locations that homecoming weekend. I'll double check to see if his current story is still what he told three years ago."

"He has to be considered a suspect until he can prove otherwise," Nolan said, his voice a near growl.

"I agree," the chief said. "But I'll also need to talk to Eric and make sure he tells me exactly what he told you—and see if I believe him."

Nolan nodded. "That's fair."

"In case you're interested, I'm still checking on the suspicion of recent fight activities," Dan said, addressing Corrie. "It's too similar to three years ago to ignore a student's comment. And Wade is helping me. He knows how that former club operated, but he hasn't pinned down anything yet. He knows some kids who were involved back then, and he plans to look them up and see what he can get out of them. If there's a new fight club, we'll stop it as soon as we find out who's behind it. It's a separate matter from our missing persons case, but I'll let you know what we find out anyhow."

"Thanks," Nolan said, rising.

Corrie started to stand, but remembered what else

she wanted to ask. "Do you have any idea where the rumor started that Nola and Swish ran away together?"

The chief shook his head. "I'm afraid not. You know how rumors are. A comment is made, and it flies from mouth to mouth. Finding an original source is like searching for the needle in a haystack."

She nodded. "I still think I'll ask around about it, beginning with the starting basketball players from that year's team."

"Ask away. I can give you a tip-off," he said, grinning at his little pun. "Chuck Osborn is out of range for questioning, but I can give you some info on him."

"You've talked to him recently?"

"It's been a while, but I can tell you he didn't enlist to get out of town because of those disappearances. His parents pressured him into it to get him away from his girlfriend when they found out she was pregnant."

"Do you know how Chuck felt about that?" Nolan asked. "I always thought he was a good kid, not the kind to leave his girl in the lurch."

"He was a good kid," Dan confirmed. "But he couldn't handle the pressure of his parents."

"They don't think the girl is good enough for him?" Corrie asked, recalling the somewhat wealthy and socially conscious Osborn couple. "Or was there money involved? Or both?"

"Both. They don't get along with the girl's parents, and Chuck is in line for a nice inheritance—if they don't change their will, as threatened. I got this out of him one day when he was in town on leave and I ran into him at the auto body shop."

Corrie started to ask another question, but the

chief wasn't finished.

"I probably shouldn't tell you this part," Dan continued. "I also talked to the girl not long ago, and she told me that when Chuck discharges from the military, he's coming to get her and the little boy she had. They're going to get married and move away from here. She didn't say where, and I didn't ask."

Corrie nodded, while observing Nolan doing the same.

"You're confident Chuck was focused on his personal problems and had nothing to do with his teammate's disappearance," Nolan said in quiet confidence.

"I am," the chief responded.

Another girl came to Corrie's mind. "What about Swish's girlfriend? Are you as sure of her innocence?"

"Her timeline is a little vague, but everyone we've talked to said she was in the gym during the party, and they assume she left when everyone else did, which would have been a little after ten thirty."

"I think I'd like to talk to Taylor, Wade and Jason again anyhow and see if they have any idea where the runaway rumor started," Corrie said, standing. "Thanks for being open with us."

"Nolan and I asked you to do this. I owe you my support," the chief said, also rising. "Call if you have questions."

~

"Do you feel like going grocery shopping?" Nolan asked as they settled into his vehicle.

Corrie grinned. "How did you guess?"

"I'm learning how you think," he said, starting the engine.

The chat with Taylor inside the store yielded no source of the runaway rumor.

"That was a dead end," Nolan said as he and Corrie returned to his SUV minutes later.

She shrugged. "It was worth checking. Kent said that's how it is in detective work. You follow every lead or idea. Some get results. Some don't."

He heaved a sigh. "Taylor said Jason isn't in town this weekend, and the chief said Wade is checking about the fights. I don't know anything more we can do right now."

"I need to do some laundry," she said, a direct hint to take her home. So he did.

Minutes later, he was glad to get home where he could relax. But he couldn't.

The unsolved question of his daughter's whereabouts weighed on his mind and heart. He tried to take a nap—and couldn't. He tried to eat—and couldn't.

The ring of his phone was a welcome distraction. It was Dan.

"Greg Briley's alibi checks out," the chief said the moment Nolan answered. "He was on chaperone duty at homecoming, visible sitting at the building entrance during a good portion of the evening, and then cleanup afterward."

"There goes our strongest suspect."

"I also spoke to Eric Tomlinson, and I agree that he's being honest," Dan said.

Nolan thanked him, ended the call and sat there letting his thoughts drift in circles. He couldn't see any answers at this point.

God, are you out there? he mumbled, lying back

in the recliner and staring at the ceiling.

He knew his irregular church attendance, more absence than presence, had been noted. Losing his daughter, and then his wife, had made him feel that God didn't care. And he didn't want to listen to preaching and platitudes from members, however well meaning.

But Corrie had also suffered tough losses. And she still loved God and attended church. She radiated a sense of peace that eluded him. He decided to go in the morning.

Corrie would be there.

Chapter 11

"Who are you subbing for today?" Piper asked, coming alongside Corrie as they crossed the parking lot to the school Monday morning, both wearing windbreakers and dark slacks. The overcast sky spewed a sparkle of rain, making them hasten their pace.

"Mrs. Higgins," Corrie said, frowning slightly. "Math isn't my comfort zone."

Piper chuckled. "I hear you. Hold on a minute," she said once they were inside the building.

Corrie paused beside her as she dug around in her satchel and extracted an envelope. She handed it to Corrie. "This is the list you asked me to make of what I remember about homecoming that year. I worked on it over the weekend."

Corrie took it and stuck it in her purse. "I'll look at it during my free period."

"In other words, you won't be roaming the halls questioning anyone during that hour," Piper said with a playful grin, heading toward the stairwell.

Corrie checked in at the office and was admitted into the math room. As she put her purse away, her thoughts drifted back to seeing Nolan in church service yesterday. He had sat in the back, but had waited to speak to her as she exited.

He had received a call from Mrs. Higgins early that morning giving him advance notice that she was sick and wouldn't be at school today. After Corrie agreed to sub for the woman, he had started to say more, but hadn't, leaving her with the feeling that he had been about to suggest they go eat together. But he hadn't. And she had been relieved. She needed to keep some distance between them.

But she couldn't shake the ever-present thoughts of him that continued to dog her. Good grief. You'd think she was one of these teenagers circulating the halls.

She was developing an emotional attachment, and she wasn't sure how to deal with it. Rationally she knew it needed to be nipped in the bud. They both had emotional baggage, and they needed to maintain professionalism between them.

She had just about convinced herself she had her common sense back in control when the bell rang and students began entering the classroom.

It wasn't until fourth hour that she had the free time to study Piper's notes. Her friend had created a timeline of homecoming day and evening, listing her recollections in order.

Pep rally last class period of the day went as planned. No problems.

I went home for a quick meal.

Went to the youth center to do some last-minute preparations for the post-game party.

Returned to school at six and watched pre-game drills.

Watched the game. It was well attended, and the

students well behaved.

At half time the king and queen were crowned.

The game resumed and ended about nine with a one-point win, which was a squeaker because during the final quarter there was a bad ref call, a parent threw a temper tantrum, and a technical foul was called against our team, resulting in two extra points for the other team.

The post-game party was a fun celebration of the close win.

Monday morning Nola didn't arrive to conduct her classes and had not called anyone. Teachers had to give up our free class periods to sub for her classes. When she was not reached by phone or found at home, a sub was hired for the next day.

Swish was also absent Monday. When his dad was contacted, he said the boy was supposed to have gone to his mother's, who is divorced from him and lives in a neighboring town.

When the bell rang for lunch, Corrie met Piper at the door of her classroom. "I've been reading your notes. I'm curious. Who was the parent who threw a temper tantrum?"

Piper frowned, thought lines creasing her brow. Then her eyes cleared. "It was Swish's dad." She shook her head. "Some parents go ballistic at games if their kids are involved."

How well Corrie knew that. "It doesn't matter. I was just curious."

"I'm going to the cafeteria. Care to eat with me?"

"Sure."

At the end of the day, Corrie decided she should check in with Nolan and headed to his office. But as she approached that end of the hallway, she saw him entering the front door of the building. Outside through the large glass paned windows, the line of now loaded buses was beginning to roll forward out of the lot.

"What's up?" Nolan asked, reading her expression as he approached her at the door of the front office.

As they entered his private office to the right of the secretary, Corrie pulled Piper's notes from her purse. "I asked Piper to write down her memories of that homecoming for me. She did so over the weekend, and I've had a chance to read them." She handed them across the desk to him.

He glanced at her as he picked up the envelope. "Is there something in particular you want me to note?"

She shook her head. "No, I just want you to read it and see if any questions occur to you."

He extracted the notes from the envelope, sat in his desk chair and began to read. When he finished, he looked back at her, his expression bland. "It matches what I remember reading in the police files. What bothered you?"

She shrugged. "Nothing, really. I just wondered about the parent who raised a ruckus. When I asked Piper who it was, she said it was Swish's dad. Do you think there's any chance whatsoever that Mr. Miller and his son could have had words later that night and something bad happened?"

Nolan frowned. "I remember the incident well, and I know Sheldon has a hot temper, but I can't fathom the man hurting Swish. He doted on the boy, and his athletic ability was like a personal badge of achievement. If anything, he was too lenient, spoiled the kid."

Corrie inhaled deeply. "I'm reaching. I know that. But I just wanted to consider every possibility, however far-fetched."

~

"Wait," Nolan said when Corrie reclaimed the envelope and started toward the door.

She stopped and faced him. "What?"

"I'd like to talk to Dan. Will you go with me?"

"How soon do you want to leave?"

He stood. "Right now, so I can catch him before he can leave the station for the day."

"Do you have something specific in mind to ask him?" she asked as they left the building.

Nolan shrugged and kept walking. "Not really. I'd just like for him to read Piper's notes and see if he sees anything new or interesting in them."

"And you want to ask if he has any updates," she added.

"Yep. And this is as good an excuse as any."

Once they were in the police chief's office, the man read Piper's notes and then eyed them across the desk. "There's nothing new here. But I give her credit for memory."

"You mean the detail about the technical foul?" Nolan asked.

Dan nodded. "Yes. Sheldon Miller can be a bit of a hothead at times, but he's a good businessman and supports the school and community."

"Do you think there's any chance that he and Swish could have fought, and he sent the boy out of town to live?"

Dan rubbed his jaw. "You mean to his mother. We spoke to her back then, and she was as upset as

Sheldon about their missing son. Said she hadn't seen Swish for days before he disappeared. She lived in Cape Girardeau. Still does so far as I know," he added.

Nolan's frustration mounted. "Have you made any other progress?"

A head shake accompanied Dan's grim frown. "We've found no truck yet. I haven't even been able to catch up with your shop teacher and interview him." He glanced at his watch. "I'm supposed to meet my wife at the Ozark Buffet in fifteen minutes. Why don't you two join us?"

Nolan looked over at Corrie. "Would you like that?"

She hesitated, but then smiled. "I'm hungry."

He figured the possibility of more chat time with the chief swayed her agreement. But he'd take it.

He hadn't been even vaguely interested in any woman since Shelly left him, and then died, but the frozen numbness and pain had begun to dissolve and thaw in the days since Corrie had come back on the scene. Because of her he had begun to feel alive again, not merely a robot going about his duties. It was good to talk to someone, share a meal with her and enjoy searching for answers together.

"Follow me," Dan said, glancing at his watch again and holding the door open for them to exit, and then locking it behind them. "Sandy may already be there."

When they had followed Dan in their separate vehicles to the restaurant, they found Dan's wife, Sandy, waiting in the lobby for him. Once greetings were exchanged, they went on inside, loaded plates at the buffet, and then sat at a table for four.

The conversation was pleasant and unrelated to police work as they focused on their meal. They had just returned from the dessert bar when Dan placed his fork beside his plate, took a swig from his tea glass and spoke seriously. "We've had a couple more reports from parents whose kids have come home with bruises and signs that make them suspect fighting. The kids aren't admitting it, but Wade is questioning anyone he thinks might know anything.

Nolan grimaced. "Are they high school or junior high students?"

"Mostly junior high," the chief said. He started to say more, but paused when his phone rang.

He answered and sat listening for several moments, his expression tightening. "I'll be right there," he said, reaching for his hat as he disconnected. "Sorry to run out on everyone, but I have to go."

Nolan had a bad feeling in his gut as he watched Dan walk out the door.

Chapter 12

"So what are our conclusions?" Corrie asked, glancing around the small room. She had said good-bye to Nolan, driven home for her Bible and notes, and then come here to the church for her Monday evening Bible study group. Their current topic was angels.

"Angels are messengers," someone said.

"There are millions of them," came from another.

"What makes them happiest?" Corrie asked.

"When someone gives their heart to the Lord," came from yet another.

Corrie nodded, smiling. "I've thoroughly enjoyed this study and look forward to Betty sharing with us next month on whatever topic she has selected. 'The angels of the Lord encamp around about those who fear Him and deliver them,'" she quoted in closing from Psalms thirty-four.

Motion at the doorway drew her attention. Dan had stepped just inside the room. He beckoned that he wanted to speak to her.

With a feeling of dread, Corrie picked up her Bible and notes and walked back to where he stood.

"Can you go with me to see Nolan?" he asked softly.

She wanted to ask why, but his grim expression kept her silent. "I'll follow you."

Without further words, they went to their separate vehicles, and Dan pulled into the street. Corrie's hands trembled on the wheel as she pulled out behind the police cruiser. She sensed bad news—the worst.

When they arrived at Nolan's house and parked alongside the curb, Corrie accompanied Dan to the door and waited while he rang the bell. She had wondered why he left the restaurant so abruptly, but hadn't allowed herself to think what she now sensed.

When Nolan opened the door, his gaze darted from one to the other of them, and then locked on Dan. His pupils had enlarged, but now they went bleak.

"Come in," he said, widening the opening and stepping back.

Corrie stood just back and to one side of Dan and watched as Nolan dropped onto the sofa, where she sat woodenly, his hand in a death grip on the arm of the piece of furniture.

Dan sat in the armchair facing him and beckoned for Corrie to move over next to Nolan. As soon as she had done so, he cleared his throat and spoke. "Nolan, I'm sorry to have to tell you that Nola's body has been found." His voice was strained.

There was silence for several moments as each man struggled with his emotions. The chief's expression reflected pain at having to tell a friend that his daughter was dead.

Nolan's face had taken on a gray pallor and contorted into taut lines of anguish around his mouth. "Where?" he asked in a strangled sob.

Corrie scooted closer and placed a hand on his

arm, wanting to comfort him and not knowing how. So she sat in sympathetic silence.

Dan took a breath, regaining his professional demeanor. "She was in what had been a ditch alongside a small family cemetery. It looks like it had been used as a private dumping ground and bulldozed over when it got full."

"It was on private property?" Nolan asked.

"Yes."

"How did they find it?" Corrie asked.

Dan darted a glance at Nolan, but answered. "The K-9 dog hit on a scent. The odor of remains sometimes changes the composition of soil and can be detected by search dogs for years. The one we brought hit on a section of ground, and Nola was eventually found. The forensics team is still out there."

"When?" Nolan asked.

"This afternoon," Dan said. "Her purse was found near her, and the medical examiner confirmed her identity about an hour ago. I didn't want to tell you, but felt I had to be the one do it. I asked Corrie to come with me for support—for both of us."

Nolan nodded woodenly. "I'm glad it was you. Thanks." Then he seemed to regain his thought processes. "Whose property was it?"

Dan hesitated, but then he answered. "The searchers covered a wide area around where her car was found. The Miller farm is about two miles from the river."

Nolan shot to his feet, nearly dragging Corrie with him as his arm jerked from her fingers. "You mean Sheldon Miller?"

Dan nodded and stood to face his friend. "That's

right. And you shouldn't go running out there and confronting the man. I," he said, stressing the pronoun, "will talk to him. Do you hear me?" he asked when Nolan didn't move.

Nolan restrained himself and stood staring at Dan. "You'll let me know what you learn?" The question was low and tortured.

"I will," Dan promised. Then he moved to the doorway. "Give me some time to do that and check his story. Okay?"

As the door closed behind Dan, Nolan faced Corrie. "Do you need a ride home?"

She stood. "No. I followed Dan here. He came by the church and asked me to come with him, but he didn't tell me why," she explained, wanting Nolan to understand that she had not been given information ahead of him.

"Can you stay a few minutes?"

She nodded. "Of course. Should I make some coffee?"

He shrugged. "I guess. While you do that, I'll call the superintendent and let him know I won't be at school tomorrow."

"Then you can call your son."

He stared at her, a muscle ticking in his jaw. "I can't bear it."

Please help him, Lord.

She took his hand. "I'd give anything to change things for you, but I can't. Is there anything I *can* do?"

"Just be my friend." He pulled her to his chest, breathing a moan of pain into her hair.

They stood several moments, sharing the pain. Then his head began to lower.

The air trapped in her lungs. Tears pricking at her eyes, she stepped back. "I'd better get the coffee going."

~

Nolan did a mental head shake. He had nearly made a colossal mistake, let emotional turmoil blind him. He picked up his phone from the table between the sofa and recliner, sank onto the sofa and steeled himself to make calls.

The superintendent told him to take whatever time he needed to deal with things. Nick said he would be heading to Red Ridge in the morning. Both kept the conversation brief, understanding how difficult it was for Nolan to talk—difficulty that his son Nick shared.

Nolan sat staring at the floor, until Corrie set a cup of coffee on the coffee table. How appropriate, he thought irrelevantly. But the smell of it made his stomach roll. He grimaced and looked at her. "I'm sorry, but I can't drink it."

She shrugged and perched beside him. Then he heard a sound. Looking over at her, he saw that she was crying.

"I have no words, only tears," she said softly, placing a hand over his.

They sat in silence for a few minutes, crying together. Then he summoned his voice. "Do you think Swish and his dad killed my daughter?"

Corrie's head rotated slowly back and forth. "I don't know. The question has been running through my mind. If they did, Sheldon Miller must have sent Swish out of town to hide him."

"If they didn't, Miller has to at least know something," Nolan said, anger roiling from him. "I want to talk to him."

"But you can't," she reminded him. "You promised to give Dan time to do some investigating."

"I know," he groaned. "Nick's coming tomorrow. He'll have lots of questions and want to look for answers, too. I'll stay here to be with him and keep us both in line. It'll also keep me from having to be around people and being asked questions I can't answer."

"I hope you'll get some rest tonight," Corrie said, coming to her feet.

He snorted, also rising. "I won't be able to sleep," he said, walking her to the door. "Thanks for coming."

The next two days were spent with Nick, making arrangements with the mortuary and dealing with Nola's possessions that he had put in storage after paying the rent on her apartment for over a year. It was heartrending, but it kept him from running out to confront Sheldon Miller.

Wednesday morning, Dan called and said he had received the medical examiner's report, and it showed that a crack in Nola's skull indicated she had been struck in the head with something firm and probably died of blunt force trauma.

By Thursday Nolan couldn't stand it any longer. He told his son he had to run an errand, went to his SUV and called Corrie. "Are you busy?" he asked when she answered.

"I'm at home."

"I'm going to go see Miller. Want to go?"

"I can't let you go alone, so yes."

"I'll be at your driveway in ten minutes."

He made it in closer to five, but Corrie was waiting at the doorway for him, the morning sunlight glinting off her salt and pepper hair. Wearing a coat since the day had turned downright chilly, she wasted no time sliding into the passenger seat beside him.

"He's bound to be at his car dealership on a weekday morning," Nolan said, backing up and steering that way.

When they entered the place, they spotted Sheldon talking to a customer. When the man looked up and saw them, he frowned. But then he spoke to the man beside him and crossed the floor to them. "Hello," he said, extending a handshake. His tone and smile were polite, but held an underlying coolness.

The consummate businessman, Sheldon was tall and well built, with strong features and deep-set eyes. He normally exuded the outgoing personality of a successful salesman, but today he was more reserved, and wary. "I'm sorry for your loss," he said, his tone sounding mechanical. "Your daughter was a good woman and teacher."

Nolan reined in his feelings. "Do you have any idea what happened to her?"

The man shook his head.

"Did your son kill my daughter, and then you sent him away to hide him?" The accusation poured from him.

"I did not," Sheldon shouted. "I'm missing my son, and your daughter is found on my property. I'm as upset and mystified as you. Now get out of here." He jabbed a finger toward the door.

Nolan clenched his fists, not wanting a fight, but ready to defend himself if attacked. "I'm going—to your property to see the place where Nola was found."

Corrie tugged at his arm. "Let's go," she said

softly. He knew she hated his behavior, yet sympathy flowed from her.

When they arrived at the Miller farm, a large modern home with extensive acreage surrounding it, Nolan parked at the edge of the yard. As he did, a pickup came barreling up behind them and shot into the driveway.

"You're not traipsing around my property without supervision," Sheldon Miller shouted as he emerged from the truck and slammed the door. He pointed to the right. "It's that way."

They hiked across a field to where tombstones of a small cemetery appeared in front of the woods. In angry strides Miller led them along a path into the woods where the trees had begun to turn from summer green to fall colors. Soon they saw yellow crime scene tape surrounding a large pile of garbage that had been strewn and dumped into smaller piles.

Miller stopped, folded his arms across his chest and stood guard while they approached the site.

Nolan walked over to what appeared the most likely dump site and stood frozen, staring at where Nola had lain for almost three years. In his peripheral vision he saw Corrie walking the perimeter of the mess.

She stepped up onto a big rock and stood gazing around for several moments, studying their surroundings. Then she stepped down and moved on to a spot near a clump of grass. She leaned over. When she came upright, she held something in her hand.

"What is it?" Nolan asked, walking over beside her.

She faced him, ignoring Miller, who had followed them. Then she held out her hand.

Nolan found himself inhaling the scent of damp moss and dirt and studying a dirty, muck incrusted broken strap of knitted cotton fabric with a clip on the end of it. "It's a lanyard," he said.

Chapter 13

Corrie examined the filthy item. It was deeply stained, but she thought it had once been red and black. "It looks like it's our school colors, and lanyards were one of the souvenir items handed out at homecoming. I think I'll take it to Dan."

Still ignoring their bodyguard, they headed back to Nolan's vehicle, Corrie being careful to not touch the lanyard beyond the tiny end of the fabric. At the SUV, she scooted inside and laid it carefully on the passenger seat. Then she rummaged in her purse and found a clean tissue. She gently wrapped the lanyard in it and buckled her seat belt as Nolan started the motor.

As he drove, she took her phone from her purse and dialed Dan's cell phone. "Are you in your office?" she asked when he answered.

"I am."

"Nolan and I are on our way there with something."

When they entered the police station a few minutes later, Dan was at his desk. He motioned to seats. "What do you have?"

Corrie took the tissue wrapped lanyard from her purse and placed it on his desk. "I found that peeking out from under a rock out at the …dump site on Miller's property," she said, hesitating over how to phrase the description in front of Nolan. "I think it's a lanyard like the ones given for souvenirs at that homecoming party."

Dan leaned forward and peered at it. "What do you have in mind?"

"Will you have your lab check it for anything that might connect it to anyone who was at homecoming three years ago."

He eased back in his chair, his demeanor conveying intense internalization. "It's worth checking. Do you have a wild theory as to who was wearing it?"

In other words, the killer. "No," she admitted. "But if it could be connected to someone, it would give us a suspect to question."

"You're as tenacious as your husband was. That's good," he said, and then changed the subject. "While you're here, I can tell you that I had a chance to talk to your shop teacher. He had what looks like a solid alibi that can be re-verified if necessary. I don't see the need for that right now, though. Our time is better spent on these new developments. I'll take this to the lab." He pushed to his feet and scooped up the tissue.

When Corrie and Nolan were back in his vehicle, he faced her before starting the engine. "I ran off and left my family, what I have left of them," he added solemnly.

"You need to be with them," she said before he could add more. "Just pull to the curb at my house and I'll hop out. I'm glad you invited me along, and I hope you'll let me know if there's anything else I can do for you."

That evening Corrie received a call from Dan. "A hair was found on that lanyard. I had it sent for DNA testing," he informed her.

She experienced a jolt of satisfaction. "Thanks. Have you called Nolan?"

"I'm going to do that next. I'm sure he's overwhelmed right now with emotions and dealing with everything, but we both know he'll want this bit of information."

"You're right. Thanks for the update."

"Have you forgotten that I'm the one who asked you to help us look for answers?"

She kind of had, her personal thirst for those answers having taken over. "I wish I had Kent's training and insight, but I think God's going to guide us. I've prayed and asked Him to do that."

"I knew you would. And I think …no, I *know* Kent would approve. He hated that he was unable to work on the case and always wanted to hear updates when I visited him."

When the call ended, Corrie took a shower and prepared for bed. But instead of going to sleep she tossed and tumbled, thinking back over the past few years. Kent had seen and dealt with a lot of ugly crimes, and he had gone over some of them with her, wanting fresh perspective. But she had never experienced this kind of personal involvement. The case baffled her. Angered her. Made her yearn for answers—and justice.

Then there had been that dream where an angel said she had been chosen.

Bible stories paraded through her mind. An angel had appeared to Zechariah and told him that his wife, who was beyond childbearing age, would have a son,

John.

Then an angel appeared to Mary and told her she would have a son, Jesus.

The two women were cousins. And both saw predictions of their angels come to pass.

Then Corrie remembered the promise in that story. The scripture said that "nothing is impossible with God." She prayed and asked God to guide them to answers that seemed impossible. Then she finally fell asleep.

Saturday morning Corrie drove to the school and found the parking lot already nearly full. She located an empty spot at the far end, parked and entered the building. Nola's funeral was being held in the gymnasium for more than one reason. She had been a member of the teaching staff, as well as her father being an administrator, and it was the only place in town large enough to accommodate the anticipated attendance.

The atmosphere of grief pervading the place was heartrending. A protective tarp covered the center portion of the gym floor where a casket occupied the left side of it. To the right was a small podium with two chairs behind it.

The east section of bleachers was packed with students, with adults to the west. Corrie recognized many in each section. Among the adults were educators and community leaders. She noted Rochelle Crocker and her mother among them. Surely, they wouldn't take advantage of this huge crowd for any kind of political campaigning.

Nolan sat next to his son in the row of seats on the floor in front of the bleachers. To Nick's other side were his wife and two children. Seeing their anguish tore at Corrie's heart. Losing a loved one was agonizing at any time, but this had to be worse.

Corrie had just found a seat in a lower tier of the adult section when Dan slipped onto the bench beside her. Deep wrinkles formed lines between his eyes. Neither of them spoke.

The pastor spoke of Nola's life and the love she had for her family, friends and students, without reference to the manner of her death. He offered words of comfort in the assurance that Nola now resided in heaven and that all those who put their lives and trust in the heavenly Father could one day join her there.

After the service, Corrie and Dan joined the line filing by and shaking hands with Nolan and his family. Nolan's hand felt cold and stiff to the touch. Corrie had never felt so inadequate in her life.

Unable to speak, she simply placed her other hand over their two clasped ones and squeezed tightly. Then she followed Dan out the door.

~

Nolan was exhausted by the time the graveside service and a meal at the church were over and they were back at the house. His son planned to leave in the morning.

Once he was in bed that evening, events of the day replayed in his mind like a reel, but Corrie's face imposed itself over all of them. He had wanted to include her with his family group, but didn't want his small family to question her presence.

Nick and his wife knew the investigation had been reopened, but not how deeply Nolan himself was involved. Or Corrie. He didn't want to worry or upset them. Nick and Annie had jobs to do and could not be personally involved in the investigation. So he figured it was best to keep it to himself.

As for Corrie, he couldn't let her burrow any deeper into his heart. He had married Shelly for love, and look how that had turned out. Now he was saddled with a staff member who had been a lover of his wife, or at least a dalliance. At this point he didn't much care what it had been.

Loving meant giving someone the power to use or manipulate you, which was too high a price. He had to maintain control, insulate himself from another broken heart experience.

The next morning he said goodbye to Nick and his family and watched them drive away. Then he went back into the house to face the darkness of his life. Tears stung his eyes.

Why, God? Why did You let all this happen?

Bitterness ate at him. He had quit going to church after Nola disappeared, but eventually returned irregularly, hoping God would speak to him there, give him answers, or at least direction. But turmoil had still reigned, and now Nola had been found—and whoever had killed her was roaming the earth free. It was beyond comprehension.

He skipped church Sunday, still wrestling emotional despair and feeling unable to be around people. But Monday morning he returned to work. He had job responsibilities, and he felt he had a better chance of learning any new information there than sitting at home. He also needed to be busy enough to not wallow in grief and a sea of questions with no answers.

Somehow the next week passed. The next Sunday

morning, he had just crawled out of bed when his phone rang. When he saw the caller identification his gut clenched. "Hello, Dan."

"Swish's truck has been found."

Chapter 14

A knot formed in Corrie's stomach when she opened the door and saw Nolan's pale expression. He stepped inside her living room and closed the door.

"What's wrong?" she asked, motioning him to the recliner.

""Divers have been using sonar technology to search the river," he said, dropping onto the chair. "They found Swish's truck in the water near a dock about a mile from where Nola's car was found."

"Something happened to him, too, didn't it?" she asked in a near whisper.

He nodded. "I think so. I have all along. Not only did they not run away together, but Swish isn't her killer. He's another victim. And he's out there somewhere."

"They'll keep looking until they find him," she said with certainty.

His fingers tapped on the steering wheel. "I want to be out there with them. But I'm not a scuba diver, and I have a full-time job that can be more than full-time."

"Did Dan say whether they found Swish in his truck?"

"They don't have it raised yet. I'd like to run out there, but I doubt they would let us get close. And I think I'll go crazy sitting at home waiting to hear something."

"It might be a long wait, but we could go to the police station and wait for Dan to get there."

He nodded. "I like the way you think."

When they arrived at the station, they found a parking spot near the empty one reserved for Dan. Nolan shut off the engine and faced Corrie. "Let's wait out here where we can see him arrive."

She grinned. "He'll know he's being ambushed."

"Right." A slight answering grin made her feel a little better about his state of mind. Nolan was strong. Looking for answers not only was a mission, but she hoped it kept him too mentally occupied to dwell fully on the horror aspects of his daughter's death.

The hint of a smile went away. "Do you have any idea who on the teaching staff or in the student body would have been angry at Nola—or hated her?"

Corrie tried to think of anyone who had caused her trouble of any kind. And all she could think of was one. "I suppose almost anyone had the opportunity and means to harm her, but the only one I've ever heard of her being angry with is Greg, and he's already been questioned and provided a solid alibi."

Pain flashed across Nolan's face at the reminder of his wife's relationship with the shop teacher. "You're right."

"What are the typical motives for murder?" she asked, trying to analyze.

He thought for a moment. "Money. Power. Jealousy. Revenge."

"Spur of the moment rage," she added. "People get into arguments, they spiral out of control and someone ends up dead. Who do we know who demonstrates that kind of anger?"

Nolan frowned. "Sheldon Miller comes to mind, but he's missing a son who has no direct connection to Nola. There's a part of me that says he has to be a suspect, but another part says he's facing the confirmation of his son being dead."

Corrie nodded. "When he followed us to the crime scene that happens to be on his property, I thought he could possibly be guilty, but somehow that no longer seems true."

"I agree," he said after a few moments.

Dan's car pulling into his parking spot drew their attention. The chief's expression was unreadable as he exited the cruiser.

They scooted out of the SUV and met Dan at his vehicle. "Was Swish in it?" she asked.

The chief shook his head. "He's still missing."

"Was there anything in the truck to tell you anything?" Nolan asked, frustration clear in his gruff voice.

Dan shrugged. "There were the usual tools, and a deflated basketball in the back seat. The only thing a little unusual was a whistle on a lanyard."

"Another lanyard, huh?" Nolan grunted.

Dan nodded. "It's probably another homecoming souvenir, but I'm sending it to the lab to see if they can determine whether it belonged to Swish or someone else."

"Like a passenger," Corrie said, thinking aloud.

He nodded again. "The fabric is so degraded

there's almost nothing left of it, but it looks like some initials scratched on the back of the whistle. It's corroded and faint."

"If there are initials on it, I'm guessing it's not Swish's," she reasoned. "One from the homecoming would have been brand new. It's not likely he would have initialed it immediately."

"I'll put a priority rush on it," Dan said. "If you're right, our suspect list grows by one."

As he turned to go inside the station, Nolan said, "Swish may still be a suspect. But if he's dead, his dad is a suspect. I'd like to talk to Sheldon again."

Dan halted mid-stride and turned to face him. "Don't do it. I'll be questioning him as soon as I take care of a couple of things in my office."

Nolan stood rigid, his hands clenched. Corrie reached over and gripped one of them. "He's doing his job. We need to stay out of his way."

"I know," he muttered in a heavy tone that revealed how much he hated the fact.

"Thanks for saying it," the chief said. With that, he went to do his job.

~

Nolan took Corrie home and saw her to her door. But he said a quick good-bye and left rather than linger as he wanted. When he arrived at his own house, he parked in the garage and went to check the mailbox.

There were several items in it. He took them out and thumbed through the stack as he walked back through the garage and entered the house. There were a couple of bills, some junk mail, and a plain envelope addressed to him that bore no return address.

He tossed the rest of the mail onto the kitchen

counter and opened the plain envelope. It contained only one piece of paper, a sheet from a small notepad. It said only:

Your daughter was killed by her mother.

His body went numb.

Then his brain slowly began to hum.

Could such a thing be true? It so, could that have been the cause of Shelly's stroke?

No way. Shelly may have been self-centered and strayed from her marriage, but she loved Nola. Of that much he was certain.

So who would make such an accusation?

The real killer. To divert suspicion, put it on someone who was already beyond human judgment. If everyone thought the killer was dead, case closed.

No way. It wasn't true.

The accuser had inside knowledge. Who knew of Shelly's indiscretions? Those with whom she "indiscretion-ed."

Eric Tomlinson knew of Nola's anger toward her mother.

Greg Briley was at the root of that anger.

Nolan reached for his phone. He needed to call Dan. But he wanted Corrie to know about this. He dialed Corrie first, and she answered promptly.

"I have something Dan needs to see. But it's late, and I know he's dead tired. And I'm sure he's gone home by now. I don't know whether to bother him or wait until Monday."

"What do you have?"

"Someone sent me a note saying Shelly killed Nola." He choked on the words.

"He needs to see it. Why don't I pick you up and

drive us to his house. He won't mind. And we won't keep him long."

The long days of emotional strain had him drained. "Thanks for the offer."

"I'll be right there."

Within a half hour she had picked him up and was pulling into Dan's driveway.

"This had better be important," Dan said when he opened the door and recognized them.

"I wanted to wait until Monday to show you this," Nolan said, extending the envelope he held in his hand. "It was in my mail when I got home. I didn't want to bother you, but we decided you would want to see it while it's fresh."

Dan took the envelope, opened it carefully and pulled the note out by the edge. It only took a couple of seconds to read it. When he looked up, his face was grim. "You did the right thing. Can you give me a quick summary of your reactions?"

Nolan drew a deep breath and recounted wondering if Shelly and Nola could have fought, something happened to Nola, and Shelly eventually had a guilt-induced stroke over it. He also mentioned thinking that Eric Tomlinson had known about Nola's anger toward her mother—and the cause of it—and wondering if Greg Briley could have found a way to silence Nola.

"I'll be talking to both Eric and the teacher again," the chief promised when he finished. "You have to let me take care of it."

Then he raked a hand over his eyes in a weary gesture. "Why don't one or both of you meet me in my office Monday morning when I'm not so tired, and we'll see if I have any new information."

Nolan frowned. "I have to work."

"That's okay," Corrie said. "I'll meet with him and then come by the school and share anything he tells me."

He nodded. "Okay."

Chapter 15

"I have two new reports," the chief said Monday morning once Corrie was seated in his office.

She watched as he opened one of the folders before him.

"I prioritized that lanyard you found at the dump site as it's related to a murder investigation," he said, glancing down at the paperwork. "The DNA of the hair taken from it doesn't match anyone in the databases."

Then he shifted his eyes to the second folder. "The lab technicians think the initials on that whistle are F. J. Does that bring anyone to your mind?"

Corrie searched her memory, picturing the whistle in her mind. "Swish was a basketball player, and whistles are used by the refs. I think we should get a list of refs from the coach and see if those initials match anyone on it."

Dan grinned. "Keep in touch," he said as she stood to leave.

Outside, it was a nice day. A light breeze wafted overhead, and the temperature was near seventy. Once in her car, Corrie pulled the teacher schedule from her purse and checked it. Coach Lorimer would be in class, but he should be in the gym. Hopefully he would step aside for a few moments and give her a quick answer.

"You again?" the sweatpants, tee shirt and tennis shoe clad coach barked when she walked through the gym doorway minutes after stopping by the office and giving Nolan a brief update. With an air of resignation he yelled to his student aide who was leading the class in calisthenics, "Carry on. I'll be back in a minute." Then he beckoned for Corrie to follow him to his office. Inside, he hustled over to his desk and grabbed the cup of coffee that sat on it. "At least your showing up gave me an excuse to finish this," he said, moving it to his mouth. He drained the cup and tossed it in the trash. "Now what is it you want?"

"I just have one question I'd like to ask, and then I'll get out of your way."

He shook his head, a slight quirk at the corner of his mouth. "But you're like a cat. You'll be back. So what's bugging you?"

"A whistle on a lanyard was found in Swish's truck. It had some faint initials on it that lab technicians think are FJ. I'm thinking a referee would be more likely than a player to have such a whistle. Can you think of any refs you use who have those initials?"

He went behind his desk, opened a drawer and pulled out a folder. "I have a list of the referees we use. I'll check it for you."

Corrie didn't have to wait long.

Lorimer opened the folder and began to run a finger down the page. Then he paused and looked up at her. "I should have thought of him. Flint Jackson isn't the best of the lot, but he's okay. I don't know why his whistle would have been in Swish's truck, but I can tell you that it doesn't seem suspicious. He's a cousin to

Swish, and I've seen them together from time to time."

With that he tossed the folder on his desk and headed back to the door. "I need to get back to business," he said over his shoulder as he disappeared.

~

As Nolan walked up the empty hallway on the pretext of being busy, he saw the door of the teachers' lounge up ahead open. As he considered a cup of coffee, Piper Randall emerged, leafing through a handful of papers and envelopes she had undoubtedly removed from her staff mailbox. When she looked up and saw him, she came marching toward him.

"Have you heard of any more new developments?" she asked, glancing around to insure they were alone.

He shook his head.

"Is Corrie subbing today?"

"No, but she's in the building."

Piper glanced at the closed gym door behind which they could hear sounds of feet pounding on the floor as students did jumping jacks. "Is she in there?"

The woman was entirely too perceptive.

Corrie's emergence through the gym doorway at that moment saved him from having to respond.

"Well, hello, guys," Corrie greeted them brightly, coming to a surprised standstill.

Nolan and Piper walked the few feet to meet her. "Does your presence here mean you're onto something?" Piper asked.

Corrie nodded. "A whistle, like the ones used by referees, was among the items found in Swish's truck. The lab technicians identified the faint, degraded initials on it as F. J. I asked Coach Lorimer if he used any referees with those initials. He does, and his name is Flint Jackson."

Piper made a little startled gasp. "Nola dated him once."

Nolan and Corrie locked gazes on her.

"Did you know that?" Nolan asked Corrie.

She shook her head. "Coach said he's a cousin to Swish."

"So there's finally a slight connection between Nola and Swish," Piper said. Then she glanced at her watch. "I have to run. My next class will arrive soon."

When she was gone, Nolan said, "These halls will be full in a few seconds. Will you meet me at the Red Ridge Restaurant about six so we can talk about this some more?"

The rational part of his brain told him he shouldn't be so personally involved with her, but another part wanted any opportunity to get information from her—and to spend time with her.

She hesitated, as if harboring similar reservations. But then she said, "Sure," just as the bell rang.

Chapter 16

Corrie knew it probably wasn't a good idea to spend so much time with Nolan, especially in public, but her agreement to meet for a meal had simply rolled off her tongue, which seemed to keep happening.

She forced her mind back onto business, drove home and had a quick tuna sandwich for lunch. Then she brushed her teeth, changed her jeans for dark gray slacks and a white blouse and drove to the police station.

When she entered Dan's office, he looked up at her. "Do you by chance have a name for me?"

She smiled. "I do. Coach Lorimer uses a referee by the name of Flint Jackson. And the guy is a cousin to Swish, which makes a referee whistle in that truck very plausible. Another interesting fact is that, according to Piper, Nola once dated the guy."

"That bears some close scrutiny," Dan said, his eyes narrowing in thought. "I'll get a search for him started. I asked Wade if he has any idea where the rumor started about Nola and Swish running away together, and he said he doesn't."

"Did you talk to Sheldon Miller and Greg Briley?"

"I did," he confirmed. "And neither of them was happy about it. I visited Sheldon at his dealership right after I left you. He clearly didn't like being questioned, but he was civil."

"You don't think he hurt anyone, do you?"

The chief shook his head. "I don't think so."

"What about Greg Briley? Being the only teachers in that building, he had a lot of contact with Nola."

"I timed it so I caught him right at the end of his last class. When I asked him about that note, he let me know in no uncertain terms that he didn't send it, and he's sick of being harassed."

"Harrassed, huh?" she repeated, visualizing Greg in a red-faced rage. "Maybe there's more of an ugly side to him than just cheating with another man's wife."

"I told the lab guys to scrutinize that note and envelope very thoroughly. But right now I need to get busy."

Before leaving, Corrie peeked into the detective office that had once been her husband's and stepped inside. Memories rolled over her at sight of the desk where their family photo had sat.

She paused and looked upward. *I'm trying to move on with my life, like you said,* she breathed silently. *I never foresaw anything like this, though.*

She firmed her shoulders and sat at the desk for a couple of minutes, just absorbing the atmosphere. As she sat motionless, she experienced a gradual settling of peace. Satisfied, she left the room.

Not sure what to do next, Corrie returned to her car and sat motionless behind the wheel for several moments. Then she had a thought and started the engine, still thinking. What was the name of Chuck's girlfriend? It had been mentioned, but her memory was cloudy.

While driving across town, she wracked her brain for the name. When she passed the Anderson's Car Wash, it came to her. Megan Anderson was the girl's name. And Corrie knew where the parents lived. She would go there and ask them how to find Megan.

She drove to the subdivision where the Andersons had a nice frame house and parked in front of it. When she rang the doorbell, none other than Megan herself opened the door. A tall girl, she wore her auburn hair in a ponytail.

Lines of puzzlement creased her brow. "Hello, Mrs. Wright. What can I do for you?"

"Talk to me," Corrie said, opting for forthrightness. She remembered Megan as a good student who was never in trouble for misbehavior. "I've been asked by the chief of police to assist with their missing persons case."

Megan's demeanor became wary. "You mean Swish and Miss Porter, don't you?"

"Yes."

"Chuck would never have hurt either of them," she said, meeting Corrie's gaze without flinching. "But I think something bad happened to those two, and I want you to find justice for them. I'd invite you in, but I was getting ready to leave for work."

Corrie took her leave. She hadn't gotten any information, but the brief meeting with Megan had given her the sense that Chuck had left town because his parents insisted, not because he was running away after committing a crime.

She had to hurry if she was going to meet Nolan

at the restaurant by the time he expected her.

~

Nolan faced Corrie across the table, fascinated by the intensity of Corrie's dark brown eyes. There was resolve there, and her voice rang with conviction when she spoke of finding Nola's killer. For a fleeting moment he was overcome with an urge to reach across the table and grasp her hand. He mentally gave his head a shake to banish the thoughts that had stolen into the mix.

Dan said they haven't been able to locate Flint Jackson."

Nolan lifted his coffee cup and eyed her over the rim of it as he drank. When he put it down, he leaned forward. "This is a terrible situation, but I sense that you're enjoying reconnecting with former colleagues and old friends."

Her head tilted slightly, and she met his gaze. "I am. I feel that I've begun a new chapter in my life. I want justice for Nola, and for Swish, since I'm afraid they suffered the same fate. But I have a sense of purpose again, the means to be of service."

He nodded. "That's good."

As they continued their meal, he watched her. And the expressions flitting across her face as she ate made him think something was bothering her. He wanted to ask about it, but sensed he should give her time to work out whatever it was.

It wasn't until they finished dessert that she seemed to have done that. "Something Piper said keeps coming back to my mind," she said, placing her fork beside the empty dessert dish.

"Which time would that be?"

She grinned at the reminder that she and Piper had lots of conversations. "The one when she said a student made a crack about someone being flattened at the flats. And Dina Eaton had said something similar earlier. I'm not sure if those comments were about the fights that seemed to be arranged events, or what relevance there could be if it was."

"Do you think that remark was a reference to Red Ridge Flats?"

"That's my logical assumption."

Red Ridge Flats was a parcel of land behind the city park where an expanse of smooth flat rocks covered nearly an acre of land. The town held their Redbud Festival there every spring.

Nolan glanced at his watch. "It won't be dark for about an hour. Would you like to run out there for a bit? Maybe it'll stir the brain matter enough to put the question to rest—or point you toward something."

She reached for her purse. "Let's go. I'll drive and bring you back for your wheels."

Chapter 17

Red Ridge Flats was surrounded by a backdrop of fall foliage turning brilliant shades of reds, oranges and yellows. Foot paths lined the perimeter of the huge tableland of flat rocks covering the ground like a monstrous rug. A stage and display booths were erected on them during each year's spring festival when the woods in the background would be ablaze with blooming redbud trees.

Nothing was held here in the fall and summer, but the litter-covered area looked as if it had been the site of private parties.

Corrie frowned at the spread of beer cans and debris. "It looks like this has become a regular party spot. I suppose they know they're trespassing, but like the thrill of sneaking in and not getting caught. This is more secluded than the regular park," she observed, visualizing their hike across the park and the open ground between it and this spot. That open field would be filled with parked cars during the festival.

She hated to think what all happened at the parties out here. Drinking went hand in hand with too many other things.

"Look at this."

Corrie turned to face Nolan, who had been walking around the area. He held up a dirty handkerchief. "Is that mud or blood stains on it?" she asked, walking toward him.

He dangled it from his fingertips, frowning in distaste. "I'm pretty sure it's blood. I found the edge of it peeking out from under a rock and pulled it out."

She reached into her purse for a tissue. "I don't know that it's important, and it's probably too old and degraded to be useful. But I think I'll take it to Dan in the morning and tell him about this mess. He can decide if it should be tested for anything."

Nolan cast a critical eye over the area. "I think he'll want to alert some patrolmen to this. And we'd better head back," he said, casting a glance at the darkening sky.

As she drove back to the restaurant where Nolan's SUV had been left, Corrie kept her gaze on the road in front of them. But her mind strayed to the guy in her passenger seat.

She chanced a glance over at him—and caught him watching her. It caused flutters in her stomach. She needed to keep her mind on business. "Can you think of any reason anyone was angry with Nola, or if there was any kind of rivalry with someone?"

"You mean like jealousy over a guy?" Nolan turned in the seat to face her.

"I suppose that's the usual thing," she admitted, unable to picture it in this case.

His frown and head shake said he agreed. "She had been hurt by a bad ending to a relationship in college, so she wasn't serious about anyone. She dated occasionally, but usually only once or twice. I think

Eric may have been different, but I heard her say she spent time with him because he didn't pressure her for anything beyond friendship."

"Do you blame God for what happened to her?" she asked, glancing up at the moon breaking through the clouds.

Nolan heaved a weary sigh. "I guess I blame Him for not protecting her. I can't understand such a tragedy."

"I can't either, but I know He's not to blame. He gave us freedom of choice between good and evil. Unfortunately, bad choices of some people have devastating effects on others. Adam and Eve chose to eat of the forbidden fruit. Cain killed Abel. And bad choices continue. I know it sounds trite, but we have to remember that Nola is in heaven with God."

When she pulled into the restaurant parking lot and parked next to his vehicle, she looked over at him, and noted movement in his throat that told her he was hurting terribly.

Help him bear the pain, Lord. Comfort him.

As if sensing her thoughts, Nolan reached over and clasped her hand. "I have to work on that. Right now, all I can think about is finding out who killed my daughter."

Corrie nodded. And suddenly her head filled with thoughts that had nothing whatsoever to do with the case. His face was now only inches from hers, and she could hardly breathe. He was going to kiss her.

She closed her eyes. And reopened them. Kissing Nolan was unprofessional. And it would change everything between them. She wasn't ready for anything like that.

As the thoughts ran through her mind, he squeezed her hand and released it. "It's been an interesting day," he said, scooting to the door. "We'd better get some sleep and start fresh tomorrow."

"You're right." She felt relieved and disappointed at the same time. While watching him walk to his SUV, she restarted her own engine. She wanted justice for Nola—and possibly for Swish. She wasn't sure what she wanted with Nolan.

She spent a restless night, unable to reconcile her emotions. Right or wrong, the man was now involved in her life—and emotions. And it seemed he felt something for her as well. That truth scared her too much to sleep.

~

Tuesday morning was hectic. Nolan dealt with student disciplinary issues, hardly able to deal with one before another arose. He sent a student to ISS just before the bell rang for lunch, and then he hoofed it to the cafeteria. After a quick lunch, he spent the rest of the seemingly interminable day checking his watch and wishing the hand would move faster. As soon as the buses were gone and the parking lot almost empty, he bolted for his vehicle and drove to Corrie's house.

When she opened her door, he entered and took a seat on the sofa as she sat in the chair facing him. "How did you spend your day? Did you learn anything?"

She shrugged, pushing a stray wisp of hair away from her face. "Not much. I went to the police station and read a couple of files Dan let me see. Then I came home and did internet research on everyone I could think of that we knew close to this case."

"Have you reached any conclusions?"

"No, only possibilities. I studied everything I could find on those basketball teammates, who have to be considered. There could have been some jealousy among them over Swish's star recognition, but to murder him? I can't see it. And I didn't find anything incriminating. Everyone spent most of that homecoming evening together and into the night, and all vouched for one another. Sure, they could have all been in on whatever happened, but surely their stories would have had holes in them somewhere that would have come to light by now. I didn't find any."

"What about Swish's girlfriend, Rochelle?"

"Like the others, she was at the party. Her mother says her friends will vouch for her being there, and she didn't get home until after midnight."

Nolan heaved a sigh. "If Mama says that's when the gal was home, I guess that's when she must have been there. What about the people connected to Nola?"

"Eric's verified truck routes had him out of range that evening. The shop teacher was on duty at school, along with Coach Lorimer."

"That leaves Swish's dad and cousin. Do you really think Sheldon Miller had anything to do with his son's disappearance? I get the sense he's feeling the kind of pain and asking the same questions I am."

She nodded. "I agree. He's hot tempered, but he doted on his son."

"What about the Flint cousin? How does he fit into this?"

"All that's known at this point is that he was probably in Swish's truck with him at some point. But he hasn't been located for questioning yet."

"So we're at a dead end," he muttered in

frustration.

"All possibilities are being considered. That's what Kent said has to be done. He said a detective has to look at a case from all angles—suspect everyone recently connected, plus a few who seem to have no connection. You dig up as much evidence as you can, probe until you come up with the most reasonable answer, and rely on your intuition."

"What is your intuition telling you?" Nolan leaned an arm on the edge of the sofa and gazed at her intently.

"The most common motives for murder—money, power, jealousy, revenge—don't fit. So this must have been a crime of passion, or simply being in the wrong place at the wrong time. And the cousin is on the run." She paused. "And God is telling me that He's going to help us find the truth."

Hope surged inside Nolan.

Chapter 18

The rest of the week passed uneventfully. After subbing at the school Wednesday and learning nothing new, Corrie visited her mother and had supper with her mom and aunt. Thursday morning she called Dan and learned that Flint Jackson had still not been located for questioning. That afternoon she tried to contact Rochelle Crocker, only to be told at her mother's office that Rochelle was attending classes in Cape Girardeau that day.

Friday, Corrie subbed again, and had only been back home a few minutes when her doorbell rang. Finding Jason Martin on her porch took her totally by surprise. The handsome young man, clad in jeans and a blue windbreaker, had intense blue eyes that darted over her in an uneasy manner. "Hello, Mrs. Wright. May I talk to you?"

"Of course." She widened the door opening and stepped back.

He entered her living room and glanced around nervously before being seated on the sofa. He cleared his throat and faced her when she took the rocker facing him. Then he drew a deep breath and met her gaze directly.

"I heard that the police found Swish's truck, and that you're working with them. Is there anything I can do to help you find Swish?"

She sensed sincerity from Jason and knew he had been a student of high integrity. "I would love to talk to you and ask you some questions about that time."

"That's why I came. But I want you to know that I didn't hurt my teacher or friend."

"We'll just chat," she said, wanting to put him at ease.

"I don't know that it'll be worthwhile, but I want to help."

This was an unexpected opportunity. She seized it. "Were you close friends with Swish or just teammates?"

"We grew up together and were classmates, and we worked well as teammates."

"But did you like him, genuinely I mean?"

He shrugged. "Most of the time. We were friends in general, but rivals in sports."

"Did you take a lot of classes together?"

"Some, but not too many. Our interests were different. I'm studying science. Swish planned to be a coach. Said he intended to take Lorimer's job when the man retires." A wry grin accompanied that revelation.

"Did Swish get along with his teachers?"

"He didn't cause a lot of trouble. He didn't want to risk being kicked off the team."

"What about shop class? Did he like Mr. Briley?"

Jason frowned. "It's funny you should ask."

"Why's that?" she asked when he hesitated.

"Well, one time Swish made a wisecrack about the man having a roving eye and thinking he was a

Romeo.”

"Do you know if Swish was referring to anything, or anyone, specific?”

Jason shrugged again. “No. I don’t know Mr. Briley away from school, so I didn’t give it any serious thought at the time.”

She didn’t see any point in pressing that any further. “What about other students? Did Swish get along well with them? Or were there some who resented him?”

Another shrug. “Some may have. There’s always some squabbling among people who spend a lot of time together, but not enough to seriously hurt him.”

She took a few seconds to form the next question. “Do you think someone *did* seriously hurt him?”

The young man’s expression went bleak. “I can’t think anything else. There’s no way he just walked away from everything he had going for him. And now that his truck has been found, I have no doubts left.”

"We’ve basically talked about his school life. What about personally? Did he date a lot?”

"He was a star athlete, so he was popular. He liked girls and could be quite a flirt. And he liked to party.”

"Did he hang out with his cousin who is a basketball referee?”

The young man studied her through narrowed eyes. “You mean Flint, don’t you?”

Corrie nodded, debating how much to tell him. She settled for simply, “Yes.”

Jason drew a deep breath, as if he had anticipated—and dreaded—the question. “He did.”

"I get the impression you didn’t approve.”

"It wasn't my business," he said. "But if you're bringing Flint's name into this talk now, maybe I should have made it my business. Do you think Flint did something to Swish?"

"I don't know. But I think he was in Swish's truck at some point."

Jason tipped his head, eyes narrowed in speculation. "You found something in the truck, didn't you?"

Corrie decided she had to be honest with Jason if she expected the same of him. "A lanyard with his initials was found."

"I had no idea that mess could be connected to his disappearance," he muttered, staring at the opposite wall. Then he focused back onto her.

What mess? She waited to see if he would tell her without being prodded.

"One time I noticed bruises on Swish's back and thighs when we were changing clothes in the locker room. When I asked him about it, he admitted that Flint had talked him into getting involved in the fight club."

Corrie went on alert. So there actually had been a club. "What can you tell me about the club?"

"It was made up of high school students who talked or strong-armed other high schoolers and middle schoolers into fighting so others could place bets on who would win. The bettors and the winning fighter would divide the winnings. Swish thought it might be fun, but it was worse than he expected."

"How did it work?"

Jason heaved a sigh that was a near moan. "There weren't any rules. The fights ended when there was a knockout or one of the fighters surrendered. Swish said he was going to get out of the club. I think it was shut down right around the time he disappeared."

Corrie cringed at the images generating in her mind. "Do you think he and Flint came to blows about it?"

Jason's head moved in a negative rotation. "I'm not sure what to think."

She considered another angle. "Was this a guys-only club, or were girls involved?"

"I think the girls just showed up to watch and root for the guys they wanted to win, but they took a lot of pictures with their phones."

"Swish was dating Rochelle Crocker at the time, wasn't he?"

"Yeah. But …"

"But what?" she asked when he paused.

"Well," he said uncertainly, "I saw her talking to Flint a time or two and thought it looked like they were flirting with one another."

That could have created conflict between Swish and his cousin, flashed through Corrie's mind. "What about after the homecoming game? When was the last time you saw Swish, Flint and Rochelle?"

"The last I saw of Flint was when he left the gym right after the ballgame. Rochelle was still at the party when some of us guys left early and went joyriding to celebrate our win. I don't know when she left."

"What about Swish?"

Jason frowned in concentration. "We all drove back to the parking lot and got into our own vehicles. Then everyone went their separate ways."

"Did you see which direction Swish went?"

"I wasn't paying attention to everyone

individually. I assumed he went to Rochelle's. He had said while we were out riding that he was supposed to see her that evening, and he'd better not be late because her temper was as hot as his dad's."

"Do you know if Swish actually went to meet her or not?"

He shook his head. "No. I never saw him again."

"After he disappeared, do you know where the rumor started that he and Miss Porter had run away together?"

Jason rolled his eyes. "I wish I did. That story was so juicy that it spread like wildfire. Where it first started is anybody's guess."

"Can you think of anyone who was mad at Miss Porter or had any kind of grudge or resentment against her?"

His eyes glistened as he blinked back tears. "I liked her. So did the other band members. Everybody did. The only thing I can think of that might have bothered anyone is that ..." "That she was the principal's daughter, and she would have been shown favoritism because of it?" Corrie asked when he hesitated.

Jason shrugged. "I don't think it mattered to anyone. Everybody knew Mr. Porter was fair and good at his job. But kids who get in trouble might have said things like that. I don't know of anyone who did, though," he added. "And I can't think of anything else I can tell you." He stood.

Corrie accompanied him to the door. "Thank you for coming. I appreciate your forthrightness."

As she watched Jason walk back to his pickup, she was convinced of his innocence. And that she had to talk to Rochelle Crocker again.

~

Nolan was surprised to find Corrie's minivan parked in his driveway when he arrived home from school after a long day that had included an after-school meeting in the administration office to discuss personnel issues. One of them was what, if anything, could be done about Greg Briley. They had no proof of anything that would justify termination of a tenured teacher. Reassignment seemed the only possibility, and they didn't know anywhere the man could be transferred.

Nolan pressed the remote control to open the other garage door and drove inside. By the time he parked and exited his vehicle in the wind that nearly knocked him over, Corrie stood at the garage doorway behind him. "I'm going to see if I can catch Rochelle Crocker at home. Would you like to tag along?" she asked.

"Of course I would," he said without hesitation. Not only did he want in on the visit, but he wanted to be with Corrie. He wanted to see if a relationship between them could work. They could set guidelines.

Who was he kidding? If he told her about his growing feelings for her, she would run like the wind. So where would these feelings take him? He wasn't ready to answer that question.

"Get in my van," she ordered, turning and walking back to it.

Minutes later she pulled into the Crocker driveway. He accompanied her to the door and rang the bell. Rochelle opened it moments later. And the benign expression on her face morphed into something less pleasant when she recognized them. "May I help you?" she asked, her tone stiffly polite.

"We'd like to chat with you a little bit," Corrie said more respectfully. "May we come inside out of the wind?"

The young woman hesitated, but then stepped back to admit them. After all, she had a mother running for a political office to consider. Nolan recalled that as a student Rochelle could be rather snobbish.

He and Corrie sat next to one another on the sofa. This was Corrie's party, so he would stay out of the conversation.

"A lanyard was found at the dump site on the Miller property. Did you have one of those?" she asked Rochelle.

"I suppose I did," Rochelle answered a bit sharply, "But that was three years ago. I have no idea where that thing is by now."

"What can you tell me about Swish and the fights?" Corrie continued, undaunted.

"What fights?" Rochelle snapped.

"The ones his cousin talked him into getting involved with," Corrie said, making it a statement, not a question.

Rochelle gave her a look of scrutiny. "You'd have to ask him about that."

At that moment Alicia Crocker entered the room. "What's going on here?" she demanded. "Are they questioning you?" she asked her daughter.

"Coach Corrie is," Rochelle said, a gleam in her eye.

Alicia's body language made an almost imperceptible change, from near hostile to more friendly. "I'm afraid you can't do that without counsel, Coach Corrie," she said as if she were joking, but there was an underlying bite to it.

"Then I guess we'll be on our way," Corrie said, pushing to her feet.

Nolan also stood.

Chapter 19

"Those two are quite a pair, aren't they?" Corrie asked as she backed out of the driveway.

Nolan turned in the passenger seat. "The momma is a barracuda, if you ask me."

Corrie nodded agreement and pulled into the street. "I've heard she makes a nice living from legal aid by plea bargaining and getting clients to plead guilty to lesser charges. Do you think she'll become our new municipal circuit court judge?"

"It looks very likely, with her running unopposed." He frowned. "I'm afraid Rochelle has become more like her mother since high school."

"I wonder if she's planning to inherit her mom's job at some point. No, she can't finish the qualifications soon enough," Corrie answered her own question.

"Do you think Rochelle killed my daughter?" he asked, unable to escape the question that haunted him.

She shook her head and steered left onto the main highway. "I don't know. Too many possibilities are on a merry-go-round in my mind."

"I don't know Flint Jackson," he said, jumping onto her mental merry-go-round. "But he's said to have dated my daughter, and he was apparently involved in that fight club that appears to have recently resurrected. He could be at the head of it, which is a disgusting thought," he added grimly. "If he is, he shouldn't be anywhere near the sports programs, or students."

"If he was helping run it, and Nola made some kind of connection," Corrie theorized, "could she have dated him to find out more about him and what he was doing?"

Nolan pondered the idea for several moments. "She was a curious sort. Maybe she heard about the fighting, was concerned about the students and decided to do something about it if she could. Especially if she thought a particular student was being bullied and wanted to stop it."

"And got in over her head," Corrie added. "Would she have confronted Flint if she found out he was involved in such a terrible thing? I suppose to make money wagering on the fight winners."

Nolan sat in silence for a bit, the idea making sense while making him sick. "I'm afraid she would have," he said slowly. "And ended up being killed by him."

Her expression became pensive. "Do you think there's any possibility she could have been keeping notes or records of any kind if that's what she was doing?"

He weighed the question. "She might have. She hated injustice and would have approached such a matter in an organized fashion."

As they approached the street to his house, Corrie said, "This is probably just wishful thinking, but do you think Nola might have had any private places where she would have hidden such notes if she made them? Like a journal. Did she keep one?"

"She did when she was a girl. I don't know if she continued the practice after she left home."

"Would you want to go to the band room and have another look around, like in that storage room, while the building is unoccupied?"

"It can't hurt," he reasoned.

Instead of turning onto his street, she bypassed it and drove to the school, where he used his skeleton key to enter the music room.

"I don't see any way she could have hidden anything out here and it still be around three years later," Corrie said as they viewed the large open band space beneath a high ceiling with bright fluorescent lighting. The tile flooring was arranged in three levels on one side of the room where the band sat.

The storage room was not locked, so entry was no problem. After another look at the memorial wall, they checked behind the shelves and inspected every inch of the wall space, as well as around and above the shelves. When they returned to the performance area after finding nothing, Corrie even checked inside the piano bench. Nothing. This was another dead end.

She faced Nolan, arms folded across her chest. "I guess I should take you home so you can find something to eat."

As they walked back to her car, Nolan listened to Corrie tell him about Jason coming to see her, and it brought a grin of satisfaction to his face. "Jason's a good guy. I always trusted him more than any of the other students."

When they were inside the car, he clicked his seat belt into place. "I'm so tired I can't eat. I think I'll crash for an hour or so and see if I feel like it then."

~

After taking Nolan home, Corrie stopped by the police station and told Dan about Jason's visit and the interview with Rochelle. Then she went on home.

Sunday morning while sitting in church, she felt kind of like the day, cloudy and about to rain—tears. Nolan was not in attendance, which concerned her. And it seemed she was on a treadmill regarding the case, walking but getting nowhere.

"Don't become weary in doing good," the pastor said from the pulpit. "At the right time we will reap success if we don't give up."

The words didn't strike her well. She was weary of wanting answers and not finding them.

"Ask God to give you insight," he continued. "Let Him guide you. Don't try to do everything alone."

She consciously made an effort to clear her mind and prayed. *Lord, help me. Show me what to do.*

When the sermon reclaimed her attention, she felt more at peace. And as the final hymn was sung, a new thought crossed her mind.

Nola had been active with the youth group here at the church and spent time in the gym with them. There were lockers in the small room that served as a dressing room.

Corrie looked around until she spotted the youth director. As soon as the service ended, she moved into the aisle and hurried to where Brian Greer stood.

"Hello, Corrie," he greeted her. "You look like you have something on your mind."

She glanced around and saw no one paying attention to them. "Do you have a few minutes to do something for me?"

"I'll take time," the thirty-something blond man said. He studied her in narrow eyed question. "Didn't I hear that you're involved in the missing persons case now?"

"I am. And I want to search for anything that Nola Porter might have stashed in the gym or dressing room. Will you help me?"

"Of course. What are we looking for?"

"Any kind of notes or journal that could relate to the fight club that was happening at the school during the time she disappeared."

"I see." His tone conveyed understanding.

Together they went to the locker room and examined each locker. They also checked above and underneath them. And found nothing.

"What was Nola's role with the youth?" Corrie asked. "I know that, besides directing the adult choir, she spent time with the youth group, but I don't know what her exact role was with them."

Brian started to speak, but paused and cleared his throat. "She simply volunteered her time to help me," he said in an uneven voice. "She helped chaperone activities and programs, and she ran the sound system for the youth choir."

Corrie visualized the setup. The sound system was in the balcony. "Is there any place in the balcony where she might have kept any personal items?"

Brian thought for a moment. "Extra batteries, wires, cables, speaker brackets, things like that are stored in one of those cabinets with drawers and adjustable shelves, like the ones you see in garages for tools. Let's go take a look."

They quickly made their way to the back of the sanctuary and up the stairs to the balcony.

"There it is." Brian pointed across the narrow room.

It didn't look promising, but Corrie couldn't overlook anything. So she walked over to the cabinet and pulled the top drawer open. It held cables. The one below it held gadgets she didn't recognize. It wasn't until she opened the bottom drawer that she held her breath.

There lay a red folder, the kind with flaps inside each cover. Corrie opened it and found several loose sheets inside each flap. They were handwritten.

She clutched the folder to her chest. "I'd like to look through this. My I take it with me? I'll return it if there's nothing useful in it."

Brian glanced at his watch. "Sure. My wife probably thinks I've abandoned her and the kids. Let me know if it was helpful."

Corrie drove home, anxious to examine the folder, but extremely hungry. She had been too troubled to eat breakfast that morning. Now breakfast food sounded good, so she made an omelet and ate quickly. Then she landed in her recliner with the folder.

In one pocket she found a grocery list, a practice schedule for the church choir and another for school band and ensembles. Nola had obviously been juggling her time in order to get everything done at both school and church.

In the other side of the folder Corrie found a job application that Nola had started to fill out but not completed. Had she been contemplating a job change?

There was also a to-do list that included having

the oil changed in her car and cleaning her refrigerator. The last item was to ask Corrie's husband what she should do.

What was that about? Had Nola been investigating the fight club and wanted Kent's advice?

Stymied, Corrie leafed through all the papers again. Then she noticed that one of the folder flaps bulged slightly. She slipped her fingers down inside it—and extracted some photos.

There were four of them, all of young boys and girls fighting. And the guy who stood watching from the sidelines was a face she recognized as matching the picture she had seen of Flint Jackson.

There was no longer any doubt of the referee's involvement in the fight club back then—and maybe one that seemed to have been resurrected recently.

She called Dan and told him what she had found. His response was that Jackson was no longer just being sought for questioning. A warrant would be issued for his arrest.

Chapter 20

Nolan ran a hand over his eyes and face in a weary gesture. He couldn't forget about the shop teacher dallying with his wife—or her with him. How could he have been so blind?

Thoughts of Sheldon Miller also plagued him. His gut said the man's son was dead—like his Nola. Finding Swish's truck had solidified the suspicions already building in his mind that something bad had happened to them. But what? And why?

It meant that he and Sheldon shared a terrible bond—the loss of a child.

He wished he had a better relationship with the man. Sheldon might be able to help. He knew more about his son—and his friends—than anyone.

He had to try to talk to the man.

And he wanted Corrie there with them.

But there were school matters that required his immediate attention.

He left the office and went about his duties. But by the end of the day he knew it was time to talk to Sheldon. He sent a text to Corrie.

I need to talk to Sheldon Miller. Will you go with me?

She texted back.

Where should I meet you?

He texted back.

Thanks. I'll pick you up at your house in a few minutes.

She was standing on her porch when he pulled into her driveway. She promptly came to his passenger door, opened it and slid onto the seat.

He let the motor idle and faced her. "I want to say how much I appreciate the way you always make yourself available for outings such as this. And to admit that I'm having trouble with keeping our relationship strictly professional."

His breath caught when her hand came up and cupped his cheek. The touch made him think that she was having the same trouble.

He stared into her eyes, and saw their pupils darken. His gaze traveled over her features one by one and came to rest on her mouth, his heart thudding inside his chest.

Then, in spite of the warnings in his head, he bent it and kissed her tenderly. And his heart turned over with sweet joy when she returned the kiss.

After a long moment, he pulled away and cupped her cheek. "I never expected to feel this way again. If circumstances were different, I would pursue it. But I can't right now."

"I understand," she said softly. "I feel the same way. So let's put it on hold and go see Mr. Miller."

He released her and faced forward, glancing at the clock on the dash. "Sheldon should still be at his dealership, but if he's not I'll drive out to his house."

It became silent in the vehicle. But he was very

aware of Corrie's presence. She looked good. She had always been attractive. She was smart and energetic and kept herself physically fit. Her silver-streaked hair was worn in a short, no frills style that suited her lifestyle and framed her dark brown eyes well. But he had never noticed the intensity in those eyes, or the firm set of her chin when in pursuit of a goal. She had just been Coach Corrie, a respected member of the teaching staff and the wife of a respected law enforcement officer.

Maturity had only enhanced her attraction. And though they had been friends and colleagues for years, everything had changed between them.

When Nolan parked in front of the dealership, Sheldon was visible inside the showroom beyond the plate glass window.

When they entered and the man recognized them, his expression remained neutral, but his eyes beamed a flash of annoyance.

"What can I do for you folks?" he asked as they approached, his tone business-like, but cool.

Nolan opted for directness. "I'm sorry if I've offended you in any way. I hope we can be, if not best friends, at least friends with the common goal of finding justice for our kids."

Sheldon's gaze raked over him in acute assessment. "You think my boy suffered the same fate as your daughter, don't you?" He blinked, pain etching his tight voice.

"I wish I didn't," Nolan said honestly. "But having his truck found like my daughter's car was found is just too much for me to think anything else. I'm sorry," he added.

"It's been so long," Sheldon said, his lips

quivering. "What do you want of me?"

Corrie spoke. "Finding the truth about things that happened a long time ago can be time consuming and require a lot of patience and persistence, but working together is better than separate. We need your help. Can you think of any places to look for your son that the police haven't searched for him yet?"

He shook his head. "The pain is just so unbearable that I can't think."

She placed a hand on his arm in a consoling gesture and then withdrew it. "I learned when our young son died at the age of two that God will give us an anesthetic if we ask Him, numb us enough to deal with things. I'm praying He'll do that for you."

Nolan observed a sheen in Sheldon's eyes as he focused them on Corrie. It made him extra thankful she had come with him.

"Thank you. Let me think," Sheldon said in a strangled voice. He kneaded his eyes with a hand, and then stared past them into space.

He stood there for several moments, lost in thought. Then a light slowly began to dawn in his eyes, while a look of utter desolation crept across his face.

"There's another dump site on a piece of my property," he said in a near whisper. "There's a place out in the woods the other side of my acreage near a ravine. A few weeks before Scott disappeared, I found out he was having parties out there with his friends, and I told him he would be without a truck and the cops called if there were any more such goings on. That put a stop to them."

"Will you direct us to the site?" Corrie asked.

As Sheldon nodded and walked over and sagged

onto a chair, Nolan looked over at Corrie. "Should I call Dan?"

She shook her head. "Let me do it."

Chapter 21

As soon as Dan answered his phone, Corrie asked, "Do you still have that search dog?"

"Yeah. What's up?"

She explained quickly.

"Where are you?" he asked when she finished.

"At Miller's car dealership."

"Stay put. We'll meet you there and let Sheldon lead us to the site."

"He's meeting us here," she relayed to Nolan and Sheldon when the line went silent.

They only had a ten-minute wait. As soon as Dan's and the canine officer's cruisers pulled into the lot, Sheldon went to his personal vehicle, a Ford pickup, and motioned for them to follow him.

Corrie hadn't realized how much land Sheldon owned. The area he led them to was three or four miles from his home. He turned onto a dirt lane and drove back into the woods to an open spot that looked as if loggers had cleared it. When he pulled to a stop and exited his truck, Nolan veered onto the lane and parked near him, the police vehicles right behind them.

They all convened where Sheldon stood as if frozen, his expression etched with grief. He started to speak, but couldn't. So he pointed. "Over there," his silent mouth motion said.

The canine officer and his dog took off that direction, and they followed. Their little caravan of four, Sheldon still sitting motionless in his truck, hiked across the area and into the woods, their gazes locked on the dog as it worked its way along, nose to the ground.

As the minutes passed and they made their way around the area, Corrie's insides knotted with frustration. They had fallen behind when the officer and dog disappeared over a ridge. As she and Nolan started up it, a shout came from the other side.

"Down here," the officer's voice rang out.

They topped the ridge and stared down into a trash littered ravine. The officer stood next to a mound of branches in front of a big rotted log where the dog was sniffing.

"What have you found?" Sheldon yelled, running up behind them, apparently unable to stay behind any longer.

Dan grabbed the man's arm. "Let us find out," he said, his tone gentle, but firm with authority. He looked over at Nolan and Corrie and then back at Sheldon. "Stay with Nolan."

When Corrie glanced over at Nolan and saw him step over and place an arm over Sheldon's shoulder, she walked past them and followed Dan to the mound where the officer and dog stood.

They pulled branches off the pile and tossed them aside to reveal the spot where the dog indicated—and found human remains. "We've found him," Dan said after picking up a wallet and looking inside it. "The driver's license is almost impossible to read, but the picture looks enough like him that I'm sure it's Swish. We'll have the medical examiner confirm it, of course."

Dan turned to where Sheldon had approached in spite of Nolan's efforts to keep him back. "You three go back to your vehicles and head home," he ordered. "I'm going to call the medical examiner and CSI team."

Sheldon protested at first, but then let Nolan steer him away. But he kept peeking back over his shoulder. Corrie's heart bled for the man as she glanced back at them.

The next day Corrie drove to the police station to see Dan. He told her that Flint Jackson was still in the wind, and no one had any more credible theories about what had happened to him. At a dead end, they were hoping that results from the autopsy report would arrive soon and give them some kind of lead.

Corrie was just sitting down to a meal of lasagna, garlic bread and a salad when her doorbell rang. She went to open it and found Nolan on her porch.

"Is there anything I can do to help?" he asked, weariness etched in his face.

"You can help me eat a pan of lasagna," she said, stepping back to admit him.

That brought a wan smile. "It sounds good."

"If you'll have a seat and give me five minutes to make you a salad, I'll get right on it," she said as he followed her into the kitchen. She pointed at the chair across the table from her place setting.

"All I have for dessert is ice cream sandwiches or drumsticks," she said twenty minutes later as they finished their meal.

"A drumstick sounds good," Nolan said, his

manner and expression more relaxed than when he arrived. "And another cup of coffee if you have it."

A minute later, he held up the cone from which he had just taken a big bite. He swallowed. "Do you know why these are called drumsticks?"

Corrie frowned. "I hadn't really thought about it."

"When a manager of a Texas candy company had the idea of coating an ice cream cone with chocolate and peanuts, his wife said she thought it looked like a drumstick. So that's what he called it."

She grinned. But her mind was still humming with possibilities about Swish. She didn't want to destroy Nolan's improved mood, but she couldn't ignore the subject. "Dan and his team are sifting through evidence one step at a time, but it's painstakingly slow," she said, and then popped the last bite of her cone into her mouth.

Nolan didn't respond at once, but became solemnly thoughtful as he finished his ice cream. "Do you want to talk through the case a bit, go back over everything and see if anything makes better sense?"

She shrugged. It would probably be a waste of time, but it might help. "Sure."

He put his coffee cup down and gazed past her. "At the end of March three years ago, the first I knew of Nola being missing was when she didn't show up for school Monday morning after the Friday night homecoming."

"She was last seen going to her car with a couple of tote bags right after the party, so it must have been between ten and ten thirty that Friday night," Corrie continued, scrawling a note on the notepad she had grabbed from a cabinet drawer.

"Nick's wife said after Shelly's funeral that she thought Greg Briley killed her." Nolan's voice quivered slightly.

"You started interviewing people," Nolan continued. "You talked to Rochelle Crocker, Swish's most current girlfriend, and learned nothing but that she had a confirmed alibi."

"I also talked to Will and learned nothing. Then we started hearing about fights that were going on during that time. Now we think the club that was shut down back then has been revived."

"Swish's teammates all seem clean," Nolan continued. "And so does his dad. But then …" he faltered, "Nola was found."

"We found a lanyard later," she hurried on. "A hair was found on it and tested, but there's been no match to it. Maybe that will happen soon." She hoped.

"When Swish's truck was found, a whistle discovered in it appears to belong to Flint Jackson, a cousin who dated Nola at least once. Nola's notes you found at the church seem to confirm that he's behind the fight club, and most likely her killer," Nolan said gruffly.

"But with two bodies being found on Sheldon's property, he still has to be considered a suspect," Corrie pointed out.

"Someone's running scared, though," Nolan said. "That note I got saying my ex-wife killed our daughter proves it. So does the fact that you have been attacked."

Corrie picked up their cups and took them back to the sink, her mind still spinning. As images played like a movie reel back over their conversation, she realized they had missed something in their timeline. "I'd like to take another look at the yearbook for that year. I think I still have one."

She went to the den and checked the bookcase. It was the last one in the row of yearbooks from her years of teaching at the school. She took it back to the kitchen and scooted her chair around next to Nolan. Then she sat and opened the book to the pages of homecoming photos.

They both leaned forward to peer more closely at them. Suddenly Corrie paused and leaned even closer. She pointed at the picture of the homecoming game in action that had caught her attention. "Who is that in the background?"

Nolan studied the spot where she tapped a finger on the bleachers behind the game action on the gym floor. Then he made a small sound of recognition. "I think it's Sheldon Miller and Alicia Crocker sitting together. Do you think it means anything?" .

She shrugged. "I don't know. He's Swish's dad. She's Swish's girlfriend's mom. I can't tell if that picture portrays a personal relationship, or maybe a professional one," she added thoughtfully. "She's a lawyer, and he's a businessman I've heard is rich."

Nolan nodded. "Being a lawyer, she won't answer any questions we might ask her."

"But Sheldon might tell us what's between them, if we ask nicely," she added, her brows lifting.

Nolan grinned. "It's too late to bother him tonight. How about we pay him another visit after I can get away from the school tomorrow?"

"We'll do it."

He stood, and she walked him to the door. Before opening it he turned and reached for her hand, linking their fingers together. "Corrie, I enjoyed this evening with you. Thank you for feeding me and discussing everything so openly."

She started to pull her hand away, but he tugged her toward him, his eyes darkening. Then his arms came around her, causing her to look up. When she did, his warm lips touched hers in a toe-tingling kiss. He raised his head slightly, his breath warm on her cheek. "See you tomorrow."

"Okay," she managed to say as he turned and walked out the door.

That night she tossed and turned, her mind bouncing from suspect to suspect, then to Nolan, and repeating the cycle. By morning she had no more answers than before she went to bed.

She ate a bowl of cereal, dressed and went to her van. As she backed out of the garage and stopped in the driveway to press the remote to close the garage door, she noticed a flutter on the lowering door. Then she realized there was a sheet of paper attached to it.

She exited her van, ran to the now lowered door and pulled off the sheet of paper that was taped to it. The printed words on it were chilling.

YOU'LL BE SORRY IF YOU DON'T STOP MEDDLING.

She stuck the ugly missive in her purse and drove to the police station, where she marched directly to Dan's office and placed it on the desk in front of him. "I found this taped to my garage door this morning."

He read it and peered up at her, his expression grim. "Someone is scared. That means our killer is dangerous. Promise me you won't go out investigating alone."

She drew a deep breath, half satisfaction and half fear flowing through her. "I'll do my best to travel in company."

He nodded. "I got Swish's autopsy report."

Chapter 22

Nolan struggled all day to keep his mind on school business, his thoughts constantly jumping to yesterday's events and wondering if today's planned visit with Sheldon would yield any new information.

By three o'clock he was checking the time regularly. He received a text from Corrie as he stood watching the school buses caravan off the parking lot. When he read that she would be there in five minutes, he hurried to his office and locked it. She was waiting for him when he returned to the lot.

"I can drive," he offered as he opened the passenger door of her van.

She shook her head. "Get in."

He did as ordered.

"I saw Dan," she said, once he was buckled into the passenger seat. "He deputized me, gave me a set of handcuffs and a warrant and said I should arrest Flint Jackson if we happen to find him."

Nolan grinned. "So you're in cop mode now, huh?"

She shrugged and put the van in motion. "He also said I'm under instructions not to be out investigating alone. So you're my bodyguard for today. I want to go see Sheldon again."

He kind of liked the sound of being her bodyguard, but not what it signified. "Has something happened since I last saw you?"

She grimaced and steered off the parking lot onto the highway. "There was a threatening note on my garage door this morning. It only said I'll be sorry if I don't stop meddling, but Dan says I have to take precautions."

Nolan emitted a whoosh of air. "He's right."

"He also told me he got the autopsy report on Swish. The boy's skull was cracked."

"Like Nola," he breathed in a whisper.

Corrie drove in silence until she parked in front of the car dealership and faced Nolan. "I figure Sheldon will be here because he needs to keep busy—and this is his second home."

They only saw a clerk when they entered, but the seasoned employee recognized them. "The boss is in his office if that's why you're here."

"Thanks, Glen. We know where it is," Corrie said.

When she tapped on the frame of the open door, Sheldon turned in the chair where he sat staring out through the window behind his desk. "Have you learned anything new?" His bleak tone matched his dark rimmed eyes that locked onto Nolan. Tears glistened in those bleak eyes.

"We just have a couple of questions," Nolan said quietly "They shouldn't take but a minute or two."

Corrie spoke. "We've studied the school yearbook for Swish's senior year and noticed a picture of you and Alicia Crocker sitting together at the homecoming game. Do you mind telling us what your relationship with her is?"

Sheldon's shoulders slumped, but he answered. "She was my legal counsel, and her daughter and my son dated. When she started coming on to me, it didn't take long for me to figure out that she wanted our kids to marry." He paused. "And that it was because she smelled money," he continued bluntly. "I dismissed her as my legal counsel."

"When did you do that?" Corrie asked.

He stared at her, frowning. "I had been avoiding her after realizing her true motive for literally stalking me, but she latched onto me the night of that picture. I went to my office the next day and typed a letter of dismissal. It went in the outgoing mail. What's the other question you said you have?"

Sheldon clearly wanted to change the subject, and Nolan couldn't blame him. He wanted to hear the next answer, but he left the questioning to Corrie.

"A whistle was found in Swish's truck that has the initials F.J. on it," she informed the man. "We believe it belongs to Flint Jackson and would like to talk to him, but we haven't been able to locate him."

Sheldon's head began a weary back and forth rotation. "He's my sister's boy. Do you think he was in that truck with Swish? Has something happened to him, too?"

"We're not sure what to think," Corrie said. "That's why we want to talk to him."

Sheldon studied her. "There's more to it, isn't there?"

She nodded. "We've found evidence that Flint was involved in a fight club, and that he had drawn Swish into it."

Sheldon moaned. "I didn't think this could get any worse."

Nolan could see that Corrie was reluctant to press the poor man, but she continued. "Do you have any idea where we can find your nephew?" she asked.

Sheldon shook his head. "I know Flint harbors a lot of anger, but I never suspected anything like this."

"Anger at who?" Nolan blurted, unable to keep quiet. Did Flint and Swish have issues?

Sheldon sagged back in his chair. "His dad abandoned him and his mom when he was eight. And my sister didn't help matters by talking bad about her ex in front of him. Flint became withdrawn and angry."

Nolan knew that some children of divorce did harbor anger, and that behavioral issues could result. It sounded like the fight club could be a twisted manifestation of Flint's anger. Could he have for some reason unloaded it on Swish? But what about Nola?

Sheldon had wilted to a slump, his face a study of pain and defeat. But now he came erect in the chair. "I have no idea where my nephew is, but I know he has an apartment in Cape Girardeau. I think he does some refereeing over there as well as here, and I believe there's a girlfriend in that area. You can look for him in the Northwest Plaza complex." He gave them the number.

"Thank you for your help," Corrie said, pushing to her feet. "I'm so sorry about your loss, and I'll continue praying for you."

Sheldon nodded, but remained in his chair.

During the drive to Cape, Corrie and Nolan did some more reviewing of the people they considered their main suspects and theorized about each one's motives, means and opportunities.

When Corrie drove up to the apartment complex and parked, they exited and quickly located the correct apartment. But no one answered the doorbell. After two more rings, Corrie faced Nolan. "He's either not here or just not answering. And I wouldn't have a clue as to whether his car is among those in the lot. Let's see if we can find the manager."

They located the office and approached the desk where a buxom, middle-aged woman sat staring at a computer screen.

"We're looking for Flint Jackson, a tenant in one of your second floor apartments," Corrie said, showing her deputy badge as the woman shifted her attention to them. "We understand that he referees some sport events here. Do you happen to know where any games are being played tonight?"

The woman grinned. "As a matter of fact, I do. Mister Jackson and I chatted for a minute outside his apartment earlier today, and he said the high school basketball season hasn't started yet, but he had agreed to ref a couple of junior high games this evening."

"Thank you very much," Corrie said, turning to leave.

When they entered the junior high gymnasium minutes later, Nolan surveyed the floor where a game was in progress. It didn't take long to identify one of the two refs as Flint.

"Are you going to stop the game and arrest him?" he asked Corrie.

"That could affect the game, and the players and spectators as well," she said. "Let's find a seat and let them finish."

When Corrie gestured toward the vacant bottom bleacher seat nearest the locker room, Nolan grinned and glanced up at the scoreboard. "There are only ten minutes left on the clock."

Those minutes, including some time outs, took more like twenty minutes to pass. As the players, coaches and referees filed off the floor, Corrie stepped in front of Flint. When he started to dodge her, she shot out an arm and said, "Flint Jackson, you're under arrest," while flashing her badge with one hand and a warrant with the other. "The police chief wants to talk to you about your fight club."

When she replaced the badge and pulled out the handcuffs, Flint jerked his arm away and spun around.

Nolan grabbed the guy's other arm. "She said you're under arrest. You can come peacefully or create a disturbance and bring a lot of attention onto yourself."

Flint looked around, wide-eyed panic on his face. When he recognized defeat, he wilted before their eyes. His mouth clamped shut.

Eyes followed them as they escorted Flint out of the gym. When they reached Corrie's car, Nolan said, "I'll sit in the back seat with him while you drive."

The trip back to Red Ridge was made in silence. When they reached the police station and turned Flint over to the officer in charge, he demanded a lawyer.

"What do you think?" Nolan asked once they were back in Corrie's vehicle.

She inserted the key into the ignition, but didn't start the motor yet. "I think he's guilty of being one of the ringleaders of the fight club and getting Swish involved. But I'm not so sure he killed his cousin. And I can't fathom why he would have killed Nola."

"He might know, or at least have an idea who did," Nolan said.

She started the engine and drove to the school where his car had the entire parking lot to itself. It looked lonely. Like him.

He reached for the door handle, but paused, uncertain this was the right thing to do, but unable to keep it inside him. "I have to tell you something, Corrie."

She stared at him, her face lit by the street light next to the car. Her eyes gleamed.

"I never thought I'd care about another woman, but I do. I've already failed at marriage. I was too busy. So was she. But I should have been more aware of her moods and needs. I have too much emotional baggage to love you, but I think I do anyhow. And I don't know what to do about it."

Wow. Had he really said all that?

She gave him a wan smile. "I also have emotional baggage. And I'm afraid I'm in trouble, too."

"Trouble?" He frowned, his grip on her hand tightening.

She nodded. "I never expected to have the feelings I do—and don't know what to do about them."

He absorbed that, breathing deeply. "Then how about this? Can we explore these feelings and see where they lead?"

A smile crept across her face. "Would a kiss now and then be okay while we do that?"

"You bet," he said, his heart expanding. Then he pulled her to him. And when he kissed her, she wrapped her arms around his neck and kissed him back.

He released her hand and eased to the door,

reluctant to leave her, but knowing it was the thing to do.

Chapter 23

As Corrie donned navy slacks and blazer with a simple white shirt Friday morning to go sub at the school, discouragement and fear had her feeling as bright as a burned out light bulb. She was back on the treadmill, getting nowhere. The confidence that had risen after the pastor's Sunday sermon had faded.

As she brushed her hair, a parade of random facts about the case floated through her mind. Unable to turn off the flow, she shook her head in frustration. But then she remembered from somewhere that when you hit a dead end, you should go backward. She applied a little eye makeup and thought back over the case step by step, picturing the events and suspects. She pondered while eating a breakfast of eggs and toast, and the more she pondered, the more driven she felt to find the answers.

Determination flowed through her. After so many setbacks, it was time for a comeback. She had to get proactive, lure out the killer. But she needed a plan, and right now she had to go to work.

While subbing for a science teacher, Corrie continued to wrestle what would bait a killer. Then, just before the bell for lunch rang, an idea came to her. It wasn't great, but it was something. And she didn't think killers were generally known to be geniuses.

She debated whether to bother going to lunch, but decided a salad sounded good. So she locked the classroom door and followed the flow of students to the cafeteria.

She had just settled at the end of a table when Nolan appeared and sat across from her. He also had a salad. She dribbled some Italian dressing over hers from a small packet, unsure whether to tell him what she planned to do.

Even though Nolan started eating, she saw his eyes making constant sweeps of the room, tracking activities. He was good at his job. She knew that.

"Are you going to eat that?"

The question brought Corrie out of la la land. Having already breathed a silent blessing, she began to eat.

"You're distracted," Nolan said, having stopped eating and placing his fork on his tray. "Is there a problem?"

She shrugged. "I'm stuck."

"Stuck, huh?" He grinned, but then sobered. "Is it about the case?"

She nodded. "It may not work, but I need to lure out the killer."

He went solemn. "What might not work?"

"I'm going to put out the word that new evidence has been found in Swish's sunken truck that proves who killed him—and that I know who it is."

"No," he snapped. "You can't put yourself at risk like that. Anything could happen. I'll do everything I can to stop you."

She stared at him. He was angry. "Then you'd better get busy figuring out how to do it." She surged to her feet, gathered her tray and headed to the window where trays were deposited.

Still flummoxed by the sharp way Nolan had spoken to her, Corrie was startled when she almost bumped into Piper in the hallway.

"Whoa there," her friend said.

Instantly alert, Corrie gripped Piper's arm and tugged her over next to the wall. "I need a favor," she blurted.

"Name it," Piper said without hesitation.

"I want you to put out a news flash. By way of rumor," she added, gathering her thoughts.

Piper grinned. "What kind of breaking news rumor do you want started?"

Corrie explained quickly.

By the time she finished, Piper's face had blanched. "Do you realize how dangerous that could be?"

Corrie shook her head. "I think I have to try something, and this is the best I can think of at the moment."

Piper stared at her in silence for several moments. Then she heaved a sigh of resignation. "Okay, but promise me you'll be careful. I'll mention it in my classes. I know which students need to hear it for it to spread," she added with a wry shrug. Then she glanced at her watch. "Gotta run."

Corrie continued on down the hall to the science lab as Piper hustled to the stairwell and headed up them to her second-floor classroom.

At the end of the day, Corrie sensed the gazes of

students following her as she walked down the hallway, exited the building and made her way across the parking lot to her minivan. She drove directly to the police station.

"I assume you've questioned Flint Jackson. How did it go?" she asked Dan when she entered his office and dropped onto the chair facing him.

He closed the folder he was studying and leaned forward on the desk. "It could have been better. He denies any ties to the fight club. Says it was Swish's mess. And of course he has no idea who killed his cousin."

Does he have an alibi for the window of time when those killings occurred?"

"He gave us one. That's what I'm trying to verify."

"Did he say the whistle belonged to him?"

Dan nodded. "He says he must have dropped it the last time he was in the truck with Swish. They went to a party together in Cape the week before Swish disappeared."

"If he's so innocent of everything, why has he been dodging us?"

"He denies that he was. Said he was doing odd jobs out of town. But he offered no proof. His lawyer already has him out on bail."

Corrie started to go to her office, but another question came to mind. "Have you learned anything from that blood-stained handkerchief we found out at the flats?"

Dan paused in doodling on his desk pad. "The blood type matched Swish, which makes him look guilty of being at the flats, possibly during a fight. But it doesn't prove he was running the show."

"I wish I could get a clearer picture in my mind," she said, trying to connect facts.

"There's one more detail," he said. "We didn't find any prints on those notes you and Nolan received. But we had them examined by a handwriting expert. All he could tell us is that he thinks they were written by the same person."

"Since you've made me a deputy, is there anything specific I can do?"

Dan's forehead crinkled in thought. "I guess you can study those files some more that I gave you earlier and see if you can come up with any new ideas or connect any dots. If you like, you can use the computer your husband used."

Corrie sensed a challenge. Well, she needed to be actively doing something. Reading those files again might be boring, but she was so desperate for justice at this point that she welcomed it, so desperate that she might have made a huge mistake. Starting that rumor might not have been a smart move. And not telling Dan about it was equally not smart. Considering that she had already been attacked, it could be more dangerous than she could handle—deadly. But she had needed to try something.

Moments later she sat at the desk where Kent had spent so many years. After reading through the two files, she booted the computer and searched for everything she could find about Flint Jackson.

He may have been an angry young man, but he had no police record. Dan had assured her of that. If his anger resulted in anything criminal, he had been successful at concealing it. But he had been in high school three years ago when that fight club had been shut down. He could have been one of the persons behind it then—and revived it this past year since becoming a referee and being around students again. She didn't like the picture, but her instincts said it fit.

Corrie turned away from the computer and took a notepad from a desk drawer. Then she began a list of things they knew, and another list of things they didn't know. She started with the things they knew.

1. Vehicles of both missing persons found in river.

2. Bodies found at different sites—but on the same person's property.

3. Eric, Nola's boyfriend, seems clean. Revealed her mother's unfaithfulness.

4. Mr. Briley, the shop teacher, was involved with Nola's mother.

5. Rochelle, Swish's girlfriend, has a strong alibi.

6. Rochelle's mother wanted Rochelle and Swish to marry. And maybe herself marry Sheldon, Swish's wealthy dad.

7. An anonymous note says Nola's mother killed her.

8. A memorial wall in the band storage room shows Nola was well liked.

9. Sheldon has a temper, but he has been cooperative and helpful.

10. Evidence, including blood on a handkerchief and the notes from Nola's folder, say Swish and Flint were involved in fight club—and making money gambling on fights.

11. Coach Lorimer doesn't think teammates would hurt Swish—or their teacher.

12. Swish's teammates seemed to like him, assuming Chuck did.

Now Corrie focused on the list of what they did not know.

1. Who killed Nola?

2. Who killed Swish?

3. Why were bodies found at different sites? Killed at different times?

4. Who wrote the anonymous notes?

5. In view of Sheldon's helpfulness, can he be excluded as a suspect?

When Corrie looked back over the lists, they only generated more questions. Was Greg Briley more than just an unfaithful husband? A killer? When Nola found out about her mother's unfaithfulness, had they fought, and Nola ended up dead, maybe accidentally? If so, why did Swish end up dead?

Did Shelly kill them both? Even if she had killed Nola, she surely would have had no reason, or the strength, to kill Swish. What was the connection?

Corrie rubbed a hand over her face, frustrated. She had no more answers than before. As she sat there staring into space, her gaze drifted back to the first list—and paused on the last item. Teammate Chuck had left right after graduation, supposedly because his parents pressured him into it. But what had his relationship with Swish been? Were they truly friends? Or had there been trouble there?

She needed to talk to Chuck's girlfriend again.

As Corrie shut down the computer, Dan appeared in the doorway.

"I'm leaving, so you should as well," he said. "Flint's alibi looks good, but it isn't quite airtight. He says he went right home after the homecoming game, but his phone records show him making a call from Cape two hours after he left. That's plenty of time to have committed two murders, driven to Cape, and been back home well before the next morning when a neighbor saw his car in front of his house."

Corrie didn't know what to think. Yes, she did.

"I'm convinced he was behind the fight club, bullying reluctant students into it and welcoming those who wanted the sport of it and a chance to make some money, but I doubt he killed his cousin and Nola."

Dan shrugged. "I'm inclined to agree. But we have to nail the real killer if it's not him. I'm going home."

Corrie grabbed her things and followed him out of the building. When she was in her van, she sent Nolan a text. He deserved to go with her if he wanted.

Going to see Chuck's girlfriend again. Want to go?

He texted right back.

Yes. I'm at home.

Chapter 24

As Corrie pulled to the curb in front of Nolan's house ten minutes later, he stepped out onto the porch, locked the door and was inside her car within seconds.

While buckling the seat belt, he gave her a guarded look. "Thanks for including me."

"You're entitled to pursue answers," she said, pulling back into the street.

"Your rumor is flying," he said, his voice lacking its usual warmth.

So Piper had set the tongues wagging.

"I admire your courage and motivation," he continued, "but I'm afraid you're making yourself more of a walking target than you already were."

"I don't want to talk about it," she said, steering right onto the highway. "We have an interview to conduct."

She hated the coolness between them, but maybe it was for the best. They needed to focus on one thing at a time, and right now that was talking to Chuck's girlfriend.

When they arrived at their destination and rang the bell, Megan Anderson opened the door, her young son in her arms. She stared at them in perplexity. "I've already talked to you."

"I know," Corrie said, realizing from the young woman's wan face and the whimpering child that she was fatigued. "We won't take long. We would like to go over your memories and see if you can remember anything, even a detail, that could help us."

Megan patted the child's shoulders and stepped back to admit them.

The room was comfortable without being shabby. Soft gray carpet covered the floor. The furnishings coordinated well. Megan motioned at the blue sofa and sat in a rocker facing it, the child in her lap.

Corrie and Nolan sat at opposite ends of the sofa, and his glance told her he would leave the conversation to her. "We'd like to know more about the relationship between Chuck and Swish. Did they get along?" she asked.

The young woman's face clouded. "They got along fine. If you think Chuck hurt Swish, you're wrong."

"So they were truly friends, right?"

"Yes," she said firmly, patting the restless child. "Chuck is a good guy. I can't wait for him to come home so we can get married and leave here. He was devastated when Swish disappeared, and again when I called and told him that Swish had been found."

"What do you remember about Swish and his other friends?"

"He had lots of them," Megan said before Corrie could expand on the question. "He was popular."

"What about his cousin, Flint? Did they spend a lot of time together?"

Megan shrugged. "I don't know if it was a lot, but

it wasn't unusual to see them together."

Corrie leaned forward. "Do you remember seeing them together after homecoming or any time the week before Swish disappeared?"

Megan went motionless, frowning. "Do you think Flint had something to do with the murders?"

"We don't know. We just know we have to clear or convict everyone who came into contact with the victims during that time period."

Megan drew a deep breath, her eyes taking on an introspective glaze. "That was a long time ago, and so much has happened. But …"

Corrie waited, encouraged by her memory-searching expression.

"Wait a minute," Megan said suddenly, tapping her little boy's shoulder. "There was a time that week that they were together. I don't know where they had been, but I remember Chuck mentioning that Swish had gotten his nose bloodied …something about not getting out of the way of someone's flying fist fast enough."

Corrie and Nolan exchanged glances. Then she smiled at Megan. "Thank you for talking to us. It helps give us a better picture of things that were happening back then." She started to stand, but paused. "What about Swish's girlfriend? Did he seem serious about her?"

Megan frowned. "You mean Rochelle Crocker, don't you? That's who he was dating when he disappeared. They hadn't been a couple all that long, but they seemed pretty involved, if you know what I mean."

Corrie grinned. "The new hadn't worn off the relationship."

Megan's mouth twitched a bit. "That sounds about right."

"What about that homecoming night? Were they together much then?"

Megan's brow creased. "I don't remember seeing them together. But I remember seeing Rochelle leave the youth center around …I think it must have been around ten o'clock or a little after. When I said something to Chuck, he said she was leaving early to meet her sweetie."

She paused, and then grinned. "Swish had mentioned their plans to him earlier that day and said he couldn't be late because Rochelle's temper was worse than his dad's."

"That's interesting," Corrie said with a forced grin. "Thank you for your time and conversation."

As she and Nolan buckled their seat belts a couple of minutes later, Corrie looked over at him. "Flint and Swish were together all right, but not at a party. They were at Red Ridge Flats."

"And you plan to share that with the chief," Nolan said, knowing the answer. "Then you're going to have another talk with Rochelle to poke holes in her alibi."

"Right."

~

The student sitting in a wheelchair facing Nolan's desk had a cast on her leg, multiple bruises and cuts on her arms and a big blue knot on her forehead. Knowing there were also non-visible injuries, he wanted to wince, but didn't. He felt sorry for the girl.

Cindy Morris had been in a car accident the previous weekend and had just been released from the hospital. Her mother had brought her to school to contact her teachers for home assignments and to arrange for tutoring.

As he stood to hand the girl a form to sign, through the glass window the other side of his open office doorway he spied Corrie marching up the hallway and surmised that she was heading to the gym to talk to Coach Lorimer again. Knowing Lorimer's likely reaction to at least a third interview, he wanted to grin, but restrained it.

After the student and her mother were gone, thoughts of Corrie and the coolness currently between them returned. He shook off the distraction and went on about his duties. But when he was in the hallway and saw her emerge from the gym, he impulsively walked that direction. He needed to stick close to her if he could. She shouldn't be running around alone. The rumor mill was alive and well, and it worried him.

"Are you headed to the police station?" he asked when he caught up to her.

She paused and faced him. A glance at her watch told him she was in a hurry. "Would you consider letting me take you to supper this evening?" he asked quickly. "I want to hear about any updates you have."

"It'll probably be after five," she cautioned, her gaze boring into him.

"I'll go straight home after school and wait there to hear from you. Will you come?" He hated sounding like a kid begging for something, but if it worked it was worth it.

"Do you think we can avoid anything controversial?"

He shrugged. "We can try."

"Okay. I'll text you when I'm on my way."

He watched her walk away, her stride self-assured, and wished he felt more confident about the state of things. He completed the day on automatic pilot, relying on experience and job familiarity while his mind continually drifted back to Corrie and her safety.

When he arrived home late that afternoon, he settled in his recliner and leaned back. He stared at the doorway that Nola used to come bouncing through multiple times a week to chat and share any special experiences of her day.

Her absence left a hole in his heart. He missed her so much, and hoped she had known how much he loved her.

Other memories assaulted him.

Nola on her bicycle. Nola playing her piano and saxophone. Directing the band at ballgames. Swish on the basketball court, the ball flying from his fingers to the basket.

Corrie coaching her volleyball team. He admired the way she had taken care of her husband, and the way she was now trying to find justice for Nola and Swish—even if he thought she was taking a foolish risk with this latest idea of hers.

Then a vision of the accident victim he had dealt with this morning entered his parade of mental images. Suddenly the memory of a similar accident victim in the past popped into the picture. Rochelle Crocker had come to school one day looking much like Cindy Morris had looked this morning. Her leg had not been in a cast, but the bruises and lacerations on her head and arms had looked much like Cindy's.

Rochelle said she had fallen off a horse while

riding on her stepfather's farm.

The stepfather, Dennis Stroud, and Rochelle's mother had divorced not long after that incident, Nolan recalled as his mind continued to drift. And not long after that Alicia had reverted to her former surname of Crocker.

The face of Dennis entered his mind. The man was an old acquaintance. And an urge to see him overtook Nolan—which was strange. They had never been pals, but friends who participated in community activities together, primarily school and church related.

An odd sense of unease came over Nolan. Why was he thinking about Dennis now? The man's relationship to Rochelle came to mind.

Something about that long ago accident had not seemed right at the time, but there had been no reasonable excuse to question the girl's story. Or how it could possibly tell him anything about the current situation.

Nolan closed his eyes. Was God trying to get his attention? Tell him something?

He hadn't been in close communication with God recently, having despaired of receiving answers to his prayers. But now he prayed. *Lord, show me if there's something I need to remember. Guide me if there's anything I need to do.*

When his phone dinged the arrival of a text, he opened his eyes and checked the message. Corrie was ready to leave the police station. He dialed her.

"Supper's on me," he said when she answered. "So drive on home, and I'll pick you up there."

As soon as she said she would, he grabbed his car keys.

Chapter 25

"Yes, I did," Corrie said when Nolan asked if she had talked to Coach Lorimer.

They were seated across the restaurant table from one another, having just placed their orders. And she was having trouble keeping her mind on track.

"Did you have any luck?" His expression was intense.

"I might have," she allowed. "We chatted for a bit. I had made a point of catching him during his free class period. When I asked him what he knew about Greg Briley, he was evasive, but I sensed that he was aware of the man's roving eye. It seems funny to me that I never became aware of that during my years on staff at the school."

Nolan shrugged. "I was just as blind. I don't poke around in the personal lives of teachers and staff. That's not part of my job, unless something about it interferes with their job performance. You were always busy, focused on your own duties," he added.

Corrie ignored the compliment. "Well, apparently Coach Lorimer heard and saw stuff you and I didn't, but he was reluctant to say anything negative about another staff member. But he did admit to seeing Greg with women other than his wife.”

“What did you ask him?”

“He didn’t mention Shelly, and I didn’t ask,” she said quickly when Nolan’s face went pale. “I asked if he had ever seen him with much younger women.”

Nolan remained silent, but kept his gaze on her.

“After debating whether to tell me anything, he said he had never seen Greg with a student, but he had recently seen him with a former student.”

Their meals arrived, so she waited until the server was gone to continue. “When I asked which former student, he said he had seen Greg and Rochelle Crocker at J & J’s.”

It was Jake and Joanie Dunham’s coffee house located south of town.

“I know the place.”

“I then asked if he had ever heard anyone else mention seeing them together, and he said he had heard a couple of others mention it. I told Dan about it, and he’s going to have another chat with Mr. Briley.”

Corrie saw Nolan’s jaw clench, and then a strange look came over his face. “What is it?” she asked, reaching over and starting to place a hand on his, but picking up a saltshaker instead.

She listened closely as he told her about remembering how much a student who had been in his office this morning after having been in a car accident reminded him of Rochelle after an accident she had been in when she was in high school.

“What’s troubling you about it?” she asked, sensing that it did.

He shrugged. “I’m probably just being paranoid, but Dennis Stroud and Rochelle’s mother divorced soon after that. I sensed there was something off about that situation, but could never put my finger on what. I have no solid explanation for why I felt that way."

Corrie didn't understand his unease either, and knew no way to ease it. They ate their meal in silence, but her mental wheels continued to turn.

When they returned to Nolan's car, Corrie buckled her seat belt and faced him. "Does your uneasy feeling make you want to do anything in particular, like talk to Dennis?"

He paused in starting the motor, nodding and looking over at her. "I did have an urge to talk to him."

"Do you know where he lives and have time to do that now?"

"He has a house and some acreage out toward the flats, and I have the evening free. Are you saying you'll go with me?"

"I'd like to hear if you learn anything," she said, nodding.

Nolan drove past the turnoff to the flats and turned onto a rural road. About a mile up that road he pulled into a driveway. The ranch style house sat on a hillside, surrounded by a huge yard.

Together they marched to the door, and Corrie stayed behind Nolan while he rang the bell.

When the door opened, a wan faced man stared out at them. Then he smiled. "What are you doing here, Nolan?"

"This is Corrie Wright," he said as they entered.

"I know who she is," Dennis said, giving her a handshake. "Have a seat."

The room was comfortably furnished, nice without being ostentatious, but lacking the careful attention of a housekeeper. Corrie perched on the sofa while the men took other seats. But she left the conversation to Nolan. This was his call.

"I'd like to ask you something personal," he said to Mr. Stroud, clearly uneasy. "I know you and Alicia divorced not long after your stepdaughter had a serious accident. Can you tell me what went wrong?" he asked Dennis.

Dennis looked startled. "Why do you want to know?"

Nolan took a deep breath. "I'm not sure. I guess I had trouble equating Rochelle's type of injuries with falling off a horse. And then the divorce happened. Was there something bad going on between her and her mother …or you?"

Dennis shook his head. "There was no domestic violence, if that's what you're thinking. Why would you ask something like that after all this time? Has something else happened?"

"That's what I'd like to know," he said to Dennis. "I feel awkward at bringing it up after so long, but another incident this morning made Rochelle's injures come to mind, and her mother's …"

"Controlling ways?" Dennis asked when Nolan struggled for a word.

After several moments, he nodded. "It seemed that way."

Dennis heaved a sigh that resembled a moan and looked up at the ceiling. Then he seemed to reach a decision and turned his gaze back onto Nolan. "That woman was the biggest mistake of my life. She threatened to ruin me if I ever told anyone what really happened, but it sounds like it's time for the truth to come out."

Silence reigned for several tense moments.

"We gave Rochelle a new car for her sixteenth birthday," Dennis finally continued. "She was thrilled and started running around more and staying out later. One evening Alicia got a call from her, and then took off before I could make it to the car to go with her. Later that night she brought Rochelle home and said there had been an accident and Rochelle's new car was totaled and had to be hauled away by a wrecker. I never knew Rochelle told you she had fallen from a horse."

"So what really happened?" Corrie blurted, unable to keep quiet any longer.

Dennis blinked and swallowed. "When Alicia and I married, I moved in with her and Rochelle in town like she wanted. But we would come out here sometimes, mostly on weekends. About a month after the accident, I was out here inspecting my property, and I found that car in a gully. It had some damage, but it hadn't been totaled. Dumbfounded, I confronted Rochelle about it. And Alicia walked in just as Rochelle admitted to me that she had hit a car, panicked and fled."

"Did you find out any more?" Nolan asked before Corrie could spew out the question.

Pain clouded the man's face. "I did some checking and figured out that Rochelle was the hit and run driver who left Dorian McCoy injured. He's in a wheelchair." The last was stated in a tone of tortured defeat.

"And you didn't know what to do."

Dennis nodded. "I didn't have the guts to tell the police, so I packed my bags and told Alicia I wanted a divorce. She agreed to it, if I kept my mouth shut. If I didn't, she said she would ruin me."

"Thank you," Nolan said, rising. "We'll do our best to keep your name out of anything that might develop."

"Don't worry about it," Dennis said. "The record needs to be cleared."

~

"What do you think?" Nolan asked as they settled back into his car.

Corrie frowned. "I think Dennis is feeling a lot of guilt over not reporting the truth, and anger at both Alicia and Rochelle."

His own feelings were a mix of relief and anger. It felt good to have gotten a truth from Dennis, but it angered him at Rochelle for what she had done, and at her mother for helping her conceal it. They deserved whatever the justice system meted out to them.

Corrie pulled out her phone. "I'm calling Dan."

Nolan kept his eye on the road and listened while she told the police chief what they had just learned.

When she disconnected and faced him, her expression was pensive. "He found our little piece of information quite interesting."

"So what has you looking so intense? Did he say something that upset you?"

She shook her head. "No, but he made a comment about her name popping up so much. And I agree. He's going to look deeper into her history."

Nolan pulled into Corrie's driveway and shut off the motor. "Thanks for going with me. It's been enjoyable and interesting."

"Thank you for the meal. I also had an enjoyable

and interesting time," she said, easing toward the door. She started to open it—and froze.

Nolan followed her gaze to her garage door. A piece of paper fluttered from it. "Stay here. I'll get it," he said, opening the driver door and vaulting out.

He ran to the door and removed the note that was taped there. Corrie's name was hand printed on the front of the folded sheet. He took it back to the car, slid inside and handed it to her.

She unfolded and read it. Then she handed it back to him.

YOU THINK YOU'RE SO SMART. BUT YOU LIE ABOUT EVIDENCE.

Mixed emotions ran through him. "This is just another warning. But it could have been much worse. The killer didn't come after you physically," he said in relief.

"A cage is rattling," Corrie said, putting a positive spin on it. "That means a mistake will be made."

Nolan wasn't ready for that. "You have to call Dan back."

She did, and they waited in the car for the chief to come get the note, as instructed. Once he had been there, examined the evidence and left, Nolan knew he should leave. But it was as if he had been dosed with inertia. As his legs refused to move, his gaze did, traveling over Corrie's features, taking in every detail and lingering on her mouth.

Awareness shimmered in the air. The scent of her shampoo made him breathe deeper. He wanted to kiss her again.

Chapter 26

Corrie's heart thudded in her chest. Scrambled thoughts tumbled through her head. Had she lost her mind?

She and Nolan had been co-workers, friends, for years. But there had never been anything else between them, except a couple of non-support issues. The recent development had become too strong, too fast. She had to keep it under control.

Yet she swayed toward him as he moved closer. And when he traced a fingertip along the line of her jaw, she didn't pull away. Instead, she lifted her face as his came toward her. And when he kissed her tenderly, her heart did flip flops.

After a long sweet moment, he pulled away and gently cupped her cheek. "I don't want to leave, but I must. These feelings I have for you have been so unexpected, and strong."

"You're not alone," she said, scooting to the door.

Afraid of what was happening between them, along with all the other things going on in their lives, Corrie opened the door and slid out of the car. "Good night," she said shakily and closed the door.

That night she lay awake for hours, wrestling her

jumbled emotions.

She had gotten involved in the case from a desire to help Nolan find his daughter, not to fall in love with the man.

She had loved her husband, but Kent was gone from her life. He had told her to mourn him, but not forever, and then to move on with a full life. But she hadn't been able to envision life without him. She had thought he was the only man she would ever love.

Lying there in the dark, a hand went over the rings on her third left finger, her mind traveling back through the years. She remembered Kent's unfailing support and love for his family. But his face wasn't as clear as it used to be. Her heart still bore the scars of losing him, but the grief no longer stabbed as sharply. Maybe getting involved and working had been therapeutic for her.

She stared up at the ceiling as the finality of her loss completely sank in, bringing more pain. Kent's funeral, and that of their young son years earlier, had been the hardest experiences of her life.

"I love him, Lord," she breathed softly. "And I know he's with You. I miss him, but I can't wish him back here to the pain and suffering he endured."

As she lay quiet and motionless, a sense of peace slowly crept over her. Then Nolan's face appeared in her mind. He had also known pain and loss. But she knew he was a good man, every bit as strong as Kent had been.

Then came the memory of Nolan's kisses. They had been soft and tender. And the idea no longer gave her a sense of guilt or betrayal. His faith had been tested, but seemed to be growing stronger, relying on

God more for guidance.

Her right hand rubbed over the rings again. Then, ever so slowly, she removed them and placed them on the table beside the bed.

Saturday morning, Corrie woke feeling fairly rested, considering how little sleep she had gotten. So she dressed, ate a donut and headed to the grocery store.

"Hey, wait up," someone called as she headed into the store. She looked back and saw Piper coming across the parking lot, her windbreaker flapping open.

Corrie waited at the door.

"I saw you in the hall yesterday," Piper said when she caught up to her. "I'm nosy. What were you doing there?"

A gust of wind nearly knocked them down. "Let's go inside," Corrie said. "I'll tell you while we shop."

As they worked their way along the produce aisle, she told Piper about Coach Lorimer having seen the shop teacher and Rochelle together.

Piper was aghast. "I had no idea Greg was such a womanizer. Did you find out anything else?"

Corrie picked up a head of lettuce and set it in her cart. "Nolan had some memories that involved Rochelle." She explained the association he had made and their visit to Alicia's ex-husband—and then finding another note on her garage door.

Piper tilted her head, studying Corrie. "You're making progress. You're also spending a good deal of time with the principal. You're in love with him, aren't you?"

The abrupt turn of subject caught Corrie off guard. She couldn't deny it. So she gave her friend a wan smile. "It sneaked up on me."

"Does he feel the same?"

"I'm not sure. I think so."

Piper's gaze darted to Corrie's hand. "You took off your rings." Then she gathered Corrie in a hug. "I hope it works out for you."

Corrie wasn't quite sure what she hoped. The whole situation had blindsided her.

Piper pulled back and studied her. "You're afraid something will happen to him, aren't you?"

Corrie considered the question. "I don't know if I could survive such a loss again."

"Would it be any worse than if something happened to him and you weren't together?"

Corrie froze. The logic stunned her. "You're right. But we haven't discussed anything …serious," she settled for, unable to find a better term.

Piper's phone rang before she could pursue the subject.

"What's wrong?" Piper asked, and then listened. "Okay, I'll come as soon as I grab a couple of things."

She disconnected and faced Corrie. "Hubby needs me to pick him up at the service station. He's leaving his truck for an oil change and tire rotation and needs a ride. We'll talk more about this later."

Corrie finished her shopping and went home.

Monday morning, glad no one from school had called asking her to sub, she went to the police station to see Dan. When she entered his office, he looked up from studying the paperwork on his desk.

"I'm glad you're here," he said. "I've been examining Rochelle's phone records from the time of that hit and run incident. A call to her mother pinged off the tower near where the wreck happened. In addition to these records, I've done the paperwork to look at her phone. And while I'm at it, I might as well try for a look at her mother's phone and see how their texts and photos compare. Who knows what other useful information they might hold? "

Corrie liked the brisk way the chief was handling this. "That accident doesn't have anything to do with the murders, but it speaks to character."

He nodded. "I'm afraid our all-American girl is developing a darker side. I think it's time to bring her in for questioning."

"You mean about the hit and run and Nola's murder? Or the fight club? If Swish was involved in that, she may have been as well."

Chapter 27

Nolan's mood all day was contemplative. That morning he had encountered Greg Briley in the teachers' lounge getting a cup of coffee. They had acknowledged one another with nods, but no smiles, and Greg had made a quick exit.

It had left Nolan wondering if the womanizing shop teacher had killed Nola, a terrible suspicion to have of a staff member under his supervision. He couldn't see a clear motive, but the feelings of dislike and distrust wouldn't go away.

His thoughts veered to Corrie. Did she truly trust him? Or was there still coolness between them?

They had kissed, and she had expressed forgiveness for the damage done years ago. But what about recently? Had his lack of support for her "rumor" plan cost him whatever ground had been gained?

Restless and edgy, he paced the hallways of the school more than necessary, trying to figure out the course of his life going forward.

Then his thoughts veered back to the ugliness of murder. It seemed that Rochelle Crocker was somehow involved in Nolan and Swish's deaths. If she hadn't killed them, she knew who had. But how could it be proven?

By the time classes had dismissed and students had left for the day, he was no closer than ever to a solution to the murders. But one decision *had* become clear.

Once the school buses had pulled off the lot, he went to his desk and began composing a letter to the school board. It was time to retire.

An hour later, he knocked on Corrie's door.

~

Corrie had been surprised at Nolan's arrival, but when he entered and told her he planned to retire, she found his news interesting.

"What do you think you'll do after retirement?" she asked, seated in a rocker facing where he sat on the sofa.

He shrugged. "I haven't gotten that far in my thinking. The plans I formerly had in mind no longer appeal. I may latch onto part-time work, something new and different. Or I may decide to just lie around in the sun all summer and hibernate in the winter," he added with a grin.

She returned it, and then glanced at her watch.

"Will you tell me about your day over pizzas if I call in an order?" he asked, reading her thought of food.

"It's a deal. Order a large one, and put Canadian bacon and pepperoni on my half." She settled back against the chair cushion while he made the call.

When he finished, he tucked his phone back in his pocket and leaned forward. "Tell me what you accomplished today."

"A discrepancy was found in Rochelle's alibi that Dan thought warranted more questioning of her. He invited me to go with him."

Nolan's brows rose, but he didn't interrupt.

"We checked at her mother's office, but Rochelle wasn't there. So we went to her apartment. She wasn't there either, but as we were leaving we saw her pull into the parking lot. Following Dan's instructions, I recorded the interview, such as it was, but he did the questioning."

"I take it Rochelle didn't react well." He phrased it as a question.

Corrie winced. "When told that we intended to question her some more, she told us to get lost. When Dan informed her that she could talk to us there or be taken to the police station, she went ballistic and let us know that we were harassing her. Then she demanded her lawyer."

"Harassing, huh?" His grin was wry.

She nodded. "At that point her mother's car came barreling into the driveway. I'm assuming she arrived so fast because the secretary contacted her and told her we had been at the office looking for Rochelle."

"So that was it?"

"The mother took over, but had trouble keeping her daughter quiet. When Dan asked about the hit and run, Rochelle remained silent. But when asked about being seen leaving the homecoming party earlier than in her original statement to meet Swish, she informed us that witnesses lie all the time. Her mother managed to keep her shut down after that."

Nolan frowned. "So you're stuck?"

Corrie shrugged. "Dan has done the paperwork to get both Rochelle's and her mother's phones. He wants to see if they have any texts or photos in them that correlate in a way that will help us."

The doorbell rang. "That must be our pizza." Nolan went to get it.

While they ate, Corrie's thought processes continued. "What's your take on Rochelle?" she asked, setting her Coke on the table next to her pizza.

Nolan swallowed and took a sip of Dr. Pepper before answering. "I'm seeing a hardness of character in her that I never saw when she was a high school student, even though she was a bit snobbish. It makes me think she could be capable of murder."

"But you're not certain."

He hesitated, staring at the slice of pizza in his hand. "I don't know. It's hard to think of a former student in such a way."

"Who do you think did it then?" Now she bit into her slice of pizza.

Nolan chewed and swallowed. "I don't think Wade, Taylor or Jason did it. And I can't imagine that Chuck was involved."

"What about Sheldon?" She laid the half slice of pizza on her plate.

He shook his head. "I could sense too many of the same emotions in him that I'm feeling. He didn't know where his son was any more than I knew where my daughter was. And, before you ask, I don't think Eric had anything to do with it."

She considered other possibilities. "So that leaves Flint, Greg and Rochelle. Which strikes you as the most likely?"

He weighed the question while sipping from his Dr. Pepper. "Flint is likely behind the fight scheme, and he very well could have gotten into an argument with

Swish and killed him. But he surely wouldn't have killed Nola for suspecting his activities. Unless …" He put the soda down, frowning in speculation. "Maybe she somehow figured out he killed Swish, and he killed her to keep her from calling the cops."

That was a thought that had been niggling at Corrie's brain. "It's a theory," she said. "But I still can't discount Rochelle or Greg. And those two have apparently been having an affair."

Nolan drew a deep breath, ignoring his food and soda. "The truth is, I think it's more likely that Rochelle killed Swish, but I can't imagine her overpowering both him and Nola, or even why they would have been together."

A picture had begun to form in Corrie's mind, but it was too vague to voice it. She would run it past Dan tomorrow. With that decided, she focused on eating.

When they were done, Nolan stood. "I'm glad you had half a chocolate pie in your fridge. It was a delicious finish to the impromptu meal."

She grinned. "I don't bake often for just myself, but I need a chocolate fix now and then."

When she rounded the table, he reached over and gripped her hand. "I liked the company more than the chocolate. I hope we can do this often. You're a special lady, and I don't mean just because of how you're helping with my daughter's case."

Her heart rate increased. But she realized she needed to exercise caution. "It's nice to have you around," was all she admitted.

But she didn't resist when he pulled her to him and kissed her. Instead, she closed her eyes and kissed him back. When it ended, she stepped away. "I think we need to slow down, concentrate on the case before getting so personally involved."

He nodded. "You're right."

She made a head motion toward the door next to the utility room. "Why don't you go out that way? It's closer to your car."

As they exited the kitchen into the garage, she turned on the light and pressed the button to raise the door. Then she accompanied him to the open garage doorway and stood there to watch him drive away.

As Corrie turned to reenter the house, a sound made her whirl back around. As she did, Rochelle appeared from around the side of the house and stepped inside the garage.

And she held a gun in her hand.

Chapter 28

Rochelle had obviously been lurking outside Corrie's house, waiting to catch her alone. And the twisted look on her face was venomous.

Dear Lord, please help me.

A verse from Psalms flashed in Corrie's mind. 'God will command his angels to protect you wherever you go.'

I could use some angels about now, Lord. Even if this means I'm going to heaven, I'm still scared.

"Hi, Rochelle," she said past dry lips, glancing out the open garage door. Only the empty street and utter silence greeted her.

Rochelle stood there, her dark look raking Corrie from head to foot. "Let's go for a ride," she said, pointing at the driver's door of Corrie's car. "Get in there." The order was amazingly calm—but deadly.

Should she try to run? Or brazen it out and look for an opportunity to escape?

"I said get in the car," Rochelle repeated, her voice icy.

Corrie inhaled a quick breath of panic and stepped toward the car door. Then she paused and faced the young woman. "Are you planning for us to go someplace where you can kill me and get rid of me and my car? If so, why don't you go ahead and satisfy my curiosity and tell me what happened?"

Are You and Your angels here, God? I need help.

"You should have stayed out of it," Rochelle snarled.

"I know you killed your boyfriend, but I'd like to know why."

"Yeah, I bet you would. You're nosy. And you're wasting time."

"Did he try to break up with you?"

A malicious sound erupted from her. "It was worse than that."

"I know he was involved in a fight club run by his cousin Flint Jackson. Did you know that?" Corrie asked, playing dumb.

Rochelle's laugh was more like a screech. "It's what got him killed. Now get in the car," she yelled, raising the gun and pointing with it.

Corrie froze, fear dulling her thought processes. "You killed him, not the fights," she said, looking back over her shoulder as she opened the door.

"He liked to bet on the fights," Rochelle snarled. "And he was excited that night because he'd won a nice pot of money. I didn't mean to kill him, but when he told me I was the prize for the fight winner, I saw red."

"What did you do?" Corrie asked, pausing inside the open car door, desperate to keep her talking.

"I grabbed his coffee mug and slugged him in the head with it," she shouted bitterly, and then the story began to spew from her. "It shattered the mug and threw coffee all over my carpet and stunned him bad, but he got up and fought me. So I grabbed the smartphone he had put on the table beside the bed and hit him some more. And he dropped to the floor, unconscious and bleeding. Then he stopped breathing.”

“How did you get him to that ravine?”

Rochelle’s grin had a leer to it. And words began to spill from her mouth, making it clear that she didn’t mean for Corrie to live to tell it. “Good old Mom stormed into the room right then. She wasn’t home when Swish arrived and came to my room, and we hadn’t realized when she returned. She heard us fighting and came and found us. When she saw that Swish was dead, she helped me put him in the clothing bag my prom dress came in, and we took him to that place where he had been holding fights until his dad found out and threatened to take his truck and call the cops if it ever happened again.”

“So what happened to Miss Porter?” Corrie asked the moment Rochelle paused.

Another screech-like sound echoed in the garage. “When we got back to the house and were cleaning up the mess, she showed up and asked to talk to Swish. I think she had found out about the fight stuff and wanted to grill him about it. I was in my room, and Mom was cleaning blood off the steps. When Mom told her Swish wasn’t there, Miss Porter asked why his truck was there if he wasn’t, and what had caused all that blood. Mom panicked and hit her with the Maglite she had been carrying and laid beside her.”

Corrie knew that some rechargeable flashlights were heavier than the majority of police batons and could be used for self-defense—or as a weapon.

“So Alicia killed Nola,” Corrie breathed in horror.

"And you took her to a dump site a little closer, but still on Miller's property. Then you went on with your life as if nothing had happened—except that you started the rumor that the teacher and student had run away together."

"That about covers it," Rochelle snapped sarcastically. "Then you had to come along and start asking questions and meddling, sticking your nose into other peoples' business." She stepped up next to Corrie and shoved her toward the car door. "Get in there."

~

Nolan shoved the gas pedal to the floor, trying to catch up to the car that had come speeding toward him as he exited Corrie's street onto the main drag. When its brakes squealed and it swerved onto the very street he had just exited, he had glanced back and nearly lost his pizza.

If he wasn't mistaken, the driver was Alicia Crocker. The car looked like the one she and Rochelle had driven in the parade, and his gut said she was headed to Corrie's house. He didn't know why, but he knew it couldn't be good. Corrie was in danger.

As he closed the distance between them, the car spun into Corrie's drive and screeched to a stop. He pulled to the curb a half block away, yanked out his phone and dialed 911 while running. As Alicia Crocker shot out of the vehicle and went running into the garage, he gave the dispatcher the address. "Corrie Wright is being held at gunpoint by Rochelle Crocker, and the girl's mother just arrived," he said when he was near enough to see inside the garage. "Help is needed *now*."

As he was assured that help was on the way, he

edged nearer, keeping to the side of the driveway so the light that framed the scene inside the garage didn't reveal his presence.

"I told you to stay away from that whole investigation," Alicia screamed at her daughter, her voice carrying to him clearly. "All you had to do was keep quiet. But, no, you had to start sneaking around and sending stupid notes. And now this. After all I've done for you."

Nolan scowled at the words, wondering just how much she had done. He knew how horrible some of those acts had been.

"Maybe the guilt was more than she could handle," Corrie said to the mother.

Nolan started to run up behind the mother, but hesitated, staring at Corrie as he sensed that she was waiting for an opportunity to do something.

Suddenly the moment arrived. He watched in fascinated horror as Rochelle swung her arms high in the air, waving the gun in a frantic way that had him praying it wouldn't accidentally fire. Then Corrie sprang laterally off one foot, jumped straight up and smacked the gun away in a perfect block move of the volleyball spiker she had been in high school and college.

As the gun went banging and sliding across the floor, Nolan prayed it would not discharge. He sprang onto the concrete driveway, ran inside the garage and managed to snatch it just before Alicia could get to it.

As soon as he had it in his grip, he scrambled upright and aimed the weapon at the two women now standing together beside Corrie's car. Both looked shell-shocked at the rapid turn of events.

"The cops are coming," he said just as the shrill wail of a siren sounded in the distance.

Chapter 29

Two days later, Corrie stepped inside Nolan's office and closed the door for privacy. She had been to the police station and couldn't wait until after school dismissed to share the information she had learned.

He looked up and smiled. "You have news?"

She nodded and perched on the chair facing him. "Rochelle and Alicia are still maintaining their innocence, but Rochelle's confession is in her record word for word."

"And you'll testify to it."

"I will. The night the murders happened, Swish and his friends did leave the party early to go joyriding, and returned about the time the party ended. Swish, apparently afraid of being late to meet Rochelle, went to his truck and drove straight to her house, more than an hour earlier than the after midnight Alicia said her daughter arrived home. Rochelle is now impersonating a clam and won't confirm anything, but she and Swish must have been there a half hour to an hour when everything went crazy."

Nolan just sat shaking his head.

"There's more evidence," she continued. "Dan was able to get both Rochelle's and Alicia's phones.

Rochelle's has photos of fights in it from around the time of homecoming. She's upgraded her phone since then, but transferred all her photos. It proves her involvement, which in a roundabout way led to Swish's death, and subsequently to Nola's."

"What about Flint Jackson?"

"He's been arrested and is facing charges. There's nothing to connect him to the murders, just the fight activities leading up to them. I'm not sure what all the charges will be."

Nolan sat in silence, absorbing the horrible facts.

"Alicia's phone yielded another interesting detail," she continued. "There were some calls to a number that turned out to be her auto insurance company. Remember the car that Dennis found hidden on his property? She had comprehensive coverage and reported it stolen. She collected the cash value, minus the deductible, for it."

He shook his head. "She doesn't miss a trick, does she? I also have a piece of information. Greg Briley is retiring."

She raised her brows. "Maybe he realized that dallying with a killer wasn't smart."

Nolan shrugged. "I heard that his marriage is on the rocks." With that, he pushed to his feet.

Corrie also stood as he rounded the desk and walked over to her. Then he leaned over and kissed her.

A jumble of emotions tumbled around inside her. As the kiss deepened, she pressed her hands against his chest and pulled back, breathless. "I need to say something to you."

"Not about the case?" he asked, looking into her eyes.

She shook her head. "Nolan, I care more about you than I probably should. And I'm scared silly."

He grinned. "There's nothing silly about you."

She sighed. "But I'm not sure about some things."

"You mean about us, don't you?"

She nodded. "I care about you …in a way I never imagined. But I need some time to think. I'm going to go visit my son and daughter, see if I can clear my head."

He frowned. "The truth is, I'm as scared as you are. I'm not fit to be a husband again, though. I might …"

"No," she interrupted. "You've been through so much, and it's too soon to make any sudden decisions. Don't doubt yourself. You've proven you can be trusted. But we both need to step back and evaluate what we're feeling—and what we want in our future."

He heaved a long breath. "I know you're right. But I'll miss you, even if you're only gone a short time."

"It probably won't be more than a week or so," she said, not sure if she could make it out of here without crying. She placed her arms around his neck and kissed him gently. Then she drew back, turned and practically ran from the office.

~

As the days crept by, Nolan did his job, doing his best to keep his mind from straying to Corrie. But he couldn't keep from wondering how she was doing and how her thinking was progressing regarding their relationship.

Today there had been a fender bender on the parking lot after school, and Nolan's stomach had been growling by the time the police dealt with the situation, the paperwork was completed and the damaged vehicles towed to a garage. Dan had grinned at the sound and suggested they hit the restaurant together since his wife and Corrie were both out of town visiting family. They had just arrived.

"This looks good," Dan said, stopping at a table.

They slid onto chairs across from one another and gave the waitress their order.

"Nolan, I'm deeply sorry about what you've been through," Dan said when they were alone. "I hope finding answers will at least give you some sense of closure." His words rang with sincerity.

Nolan nodded. "Nothing can take away the pain, but the memories are good. They help. Those and lots of prayer."

Creases appeared between the chief's brows. "I'm glad. Have you heard from Corrie?"

Nolan felt heat creeping up his neck, a totally alien feeling for a man of his age and experience. "I've spoken to her by phone a couple of times. She called once when she was at her daughter's. Then I called her while she was visiting her son. Both times she indicated she's enjoying spending time with them and the grandkids."

He had to give her space and time to decide how to proceed with her life—and pray that he would be part of it.

"We asked her if she'll consider attending the police academy after she returns and join our force when she's done," the chief said. "As for you and her, I think the two of you are so dumbfounded at how things have developed that you can't think straight."

Nolan studied the smug expression on Dan's face. "Since when are you a shrink?"

The man grinned. "Since I've seen the two of you together so much. You fit."

Nolan thought so too, but he couldn't pressure her.

Dan leaned back in the chair, arms folded across his chest. "You miss her, don't you?" His expression was smug.

"You're meddling."

He smirked. "I'm a cop. I study people. And I know what I see. Just being honest."

Nolan felt exposed—and couldn't think how to handle his friend.

Suddenly Dan's face went sober, and he leaned forward on the table. "You're in love with her, aren't you?"

The arrival of their food saved Nolan from having to answer, but Dan knew.

After they ate and parted company, Nolan sat in his vehicle and pulled out his phone. He started to call Corrie, but hesitated. He was afraid to dial, because he was afraid he might say too much, like tell her how much he loved her, and ask her if she trusted him enough to join her life to his.

Instead, he called his son for a chat.

Chapter 30

Corrie locked her front door and went to her car. She was tired, having arrived home late last night, but wanted to be in church this morning. She needed encouragement and strength.

Over the past few days she had stored the memories of Nolan's kiss in the recesses of her mind and focused on time with her son Jeremy, and then with her daughter Kayla. During their talks she had shared with them that she was lonely—and in love—but didn't want to do anything that would be a mistake or alienate her children in any way.

Both had assured her that they understood and were aware of their dad's words to her about moving on with her life. They encouraged her to do that and be happy.

Corrie drove up the street that was lined with trees and foliage that were changing from the vibrant fall colors to yellows and browns. Leaves were beginning to drift to the ground.

Sitting in the church service minutes later, she listened as the congregation sang *When We All Get to Heaven,* unable to sing past the constriction in her throat.

Heaven. Kent was there. She knew it.

The thought brought her comfort.

Then the pastor stepped to the pulpit and began to speak. "Life isn't always easy. The Bible doesn't promise that we won't experience sadness or hardship in our lives, but it does tell us that God is faithful and will comfort us. If we reach out to Him, we can experience the beginning of peace, healing for our aching hearts and direction for our lives. There is no earthly sorrow that heaven can't heal."

As the words sank into her heart, Corrie felt a sense of peace enfold her.

It's time to move on.

It seemed as if Kent was sending her a message from heaven.

She swallowed and blinked back tears.

Peripheral movement in the aisle drew her attention to the sight of Nolan stopping next to her pew. He slid into it beside her, and his hand came over hers. She marveled that he should come to her exactly when she needed him.

They sat in silent communication through the remainder of the service. At the end of the benediction, he tugged at her hand and led her to the doorway.

When they had shaken hands with the pastor and were outside, he stopped at the top of the steps and faced her. "Let's go for a ride. If you'll go with me," he added, the slight unevenness of his voice making her realize he was uncertain, totally unlike him.

Corrie looked directly into his eyes. "Sure, I'll go with you."

They hurried to his vehicle and climbed into it. When they were seated and he started the motor, she asked, "Where are we going?"

He glanced over at her, his expression hard to read. "I'm not sure. So long as you're with me, I don't care. Just somewhere we can talk without being interrupted."

Less than ten minutes later he pulled into the school parking lot. "Let's walk," he said, looking over at her.

They exited, and he came around to meet her at the passenger door. He took her arm and steered her toward the entrance, but then veered toward the wooden bench in front of the building. "Let's sit there."

Once they were seated, he faced her and took her hand. His gaze made her heart surge to a rapid beat, nearly melting at the sight of his handsome frame, those deep-set eyes glowing with intent.

"Have you had time to think about the future …our future?" he asked softly, a touch of tentativeness in the question.

She nodded. "I have. I've also chatted with my kids. And Dan," she added after a brief pause.

Nolan frowned. "Was it all good?"

She nodded again. "Kayla and Jeremy both assured me that they understand my feelings and encouraged me to move forward with my life. Dan says the police force, has enough funding to expand a little bit. They want me to begin formal training, join the force, and work up to detective. The position is to be in addition to the full-time person they're already in the process of hiring."

"Do you plan to do it?"

"I told him I'll give him an answer after I've talked to someone."

He grinned. "If that someone is me, I say go for it."

She smiled. "Okay, I will."

He nodded approval. "You're not the only one with news. I've talked to my son, and he's supportive of my relationship with you."

She smiled. "That's good."

"The school board is looking for my replacement," he continued. "And I've been approached about a less demanding position."

Corrie stared at him, taking in the smile tugging at the corners of his mouth. "Well, are you going to tell me what it is, or leave it for me to hear through the rumor mill?"

He chuckled. "The pastor and deacons want to start a private school at the church, and they want me to help them build and run it."

Corrie couldn't help but think God was orchestrating something here. Could it be what she hoped?

Nolan cleared his throat, his grip on her hand tightening. "After all that's happened to us, I understand that we needed time to think and evaluate our feelings and circumstances, but I'm impatient. I know we're still grieving the loss of loved ones, and I don't deserve you."

Her heart pounding, Corrie pulled her hands free and bracketed his face with them. Staring into the dark depths of his eyes, she said, "The past is behind us. Nothing can change the reality of what we've lost, and there will always be pain associated with the thoughts and memories of them, but we can go on living. And you've done everything possible to make amends to me."

His eyes burned with an intensity that made her tremble. "I want to be with you, but I'll wait if you need more time to learn to trust me …and love me."

She struggled for composure. "I trust God. And I trust you."

"Do you mean that?"

She nodded. "I'm also in love with you. I never thought I'd say that to any man again. But I'm ready for a new beginning …if you are."

When he didn't respond immediately, she was afraid she had made a mistake. But then he drew a huge breath, and a smile exploded across his face. "Does this mean you'll marry me?"

"It's what I want …if you love me."

"The reason I didn't support your plan to draw out the killer was only because I was in love with you and petrified at the thought of anything happening to you. I love you with all my heart. And now I'd love to kiss you."

She moved willingly into his arms and met his kiss halfway, knowing that God had once again blessed her with a love beyond measure.

When he drew back, he gripped her hands in his. "You can live with me in my house, or I'll live with you in yours. I don't care where we live, so long as we're together."

"I feel the same way," she said, dizzy with happiness. "We can spend some time at each place and then decide if we want to settle on one of them. Or we can build or buy something that's ours." She stressed the pronoun.

He tipped his head. "I'll be fully retired in June.

Would that be a good time for a wedding?"

She pursed her mouth in thought. "I'm so thankful, and Thanksgiving is in three weeks. Would that be too soon?"

"It would be perfect," he said, love shining from the depths of his eyes. Then he pulled her to him and gave her a gentle kiss that settled the matter.

Helen Gray grew up in a small Missouri town and married her pastor. While working alongside her husband in his ministry, she had three children, taught school, directed/accompanied church music programs, and became an amateur ventriloquist. Now retired and recently widowed, she still lived in her native Missouri Ozarks where she continues to weave stories meant to honor God and depict Christian lives and problems as she knows and observes them. Helen thanks God for the time and opportunity to write and considers it an added blessing if her stories touch others in even a small way.

http://www.helenbrowngray.com

MOZARK MARRIAGES
Ozark Sweetheart
Ozark Reunion
Ozark Wedding
Mozark Marriages Boxed Set
DODGE CITY DUOS
Bandit Bride
Prairie Bride
Dodge City Duos Boxed Set
HEARTLAND HEARTMATES
Show Me Love
Heartland Illusions
Mozark Vision
Missouri Catch

Heartland Heartmates Boxed Set
BOOTHEEL BRIDES
Bootheel Bride
Bootheel Bachelor
Bootheel Betrothal
Bootheel Brides Boxed Set
LAKE OZARK LADIES
Paige's Proposal
Brooke's Bargain
Haley's Hero
Kelsey's Keeper
Lake Ozark Ladies Boxed Set
HEARTLAND HEARTSTOPPERS
Schoolhouse Justice
Small Town Injustice
Workplace Danger
OZARK HILLS HOMICIDE
Complex Conspiracy
Cold Case Complicity
Cold Case Complicity

NOVELLAS
Hawthorne Hope
Tree of Hope
River Town Romance (2 in 1)
Pasque Plight
Black-Eyed Susan's Secret
Love Blooms (2 in 1)
Shamrock Ruby
Dream Team
Mother Road Matches (2 in 1)
Secrets in the Park
Secrets of the Heart (5 in 1)
Gift Bride
A Time to Love
MYSTERIES

HELEN GRAY

<u>Educated in Murder</u>
<u>Preyed in Murder</u>
<u>Coached in Murder</u>
<u>Rivaled in Murder</u>
<u>Keyed in Murder</u>
<u>Tutored in Murder</u>